LIGHT &
SHADOW

LIGHT &
SHADOW

MINDS SHINE BRIGHT
INTERNATIONAL CREATIVE
WRITING ANTHOLOGY
SEASONS 2 2025

MSB
MINDS SHINE BRIGHT

Editor: Amanda Scotney
writing@mindsshinebright.com

Published by Minds Shine Bright 2025
PO Box 1042
Windsor, 3181, VIC, Australia
Website: www.mindsshinebright.com
Subscribe: www.mindsshinebright.com/minds-shine-bright-blog
Book design and layout by Ampersand Duck
Cover photograph by Amanda Scotney
Printed by IngramSpark

A catalogue record for this
book is available from the
National Library of Australia

ISBN 978-0-6455231-6-4

The views expressed by Minds Shine Bright contributors are not necessarily
those of the editors or publisher.

Minds Shine Bright acknowledges the people of the Kulin Nation, the Traditional Custodians
of the land on which we live and work and where we have created this anthology. We pay
respects to their long history and culture, and their Elders
past and present.

Special thanks to my friends and family and partner Tony who have supported and
encouraged me and to the libraries, schools, and arts and writers' organisations that help
reading writing to flourish; and to all the book partners that have helped to promote the
Minds Shine Bright writing competitions, workshops and books. Thanks to all the writers,
poets and screenwriters who have submitted their work
to Minds Shine Bright.

This publication includes strong themes, images and language that may
be confronting for some readers. Parental guidance is recommended for
young adult readers.

CONTENTS

INTRODUCTION

AMANDA SCOTNEY

Light and Shadow anthology is sublimely dark and light with moments of illumination. Everyday life is shown to be complex and beautiful, with touching and fragile moments. By examining and exploring the shadows, darkness and variations of light that create the external world and our inner selves we can learn, reflect, endure, survive, grieve and experience moments of inspiration or transcendence.

Light and Shadow is a curated collection of short stories, poems and flash fiction featuring the winning and commended entries from the Minds Shine Bright writing competition. It is the second anthology in the Seasons Series, that explores themes relating to the external environment, bringing together writers and poets from Australia, Ireland, the United Kingdom, Canada, the United States and New Zealand.

Light and Shadow starts with the *Top Eleven* pieces. First Prize winner Isi Unikowski's poem, 'Bright Square of Morning' takes an everyday journey and transforms it into something memorable, universal and gently uplifting. Helen Booth's 'The Brightest Star' is a warm and enduring story about love and photography at the beach on cold winter's nights. It is inspired by the photography of Craig Crosswaite and dedicated to Helen's late partner Alan Bland. 'Roots' by American indigenous writer Edie Redwine is a visceral tale of survival and connection to the spirits of the land. 'Slither of Light', a poem by Paul Drewitt, captures the terror of a young boy's nightmares. A troll is a metaphor for the hidden abuse that many children suffer. This poem should be read together with Angela Costi's poem 'Medicinal' (a response to Mary Oliver's poetry, in particular 'The Summer Day' (1990)) which explores child abuse, family violence and the transformative power of poetry.

In 'Cash Only' by Gayle Beveridge, the protagonist who can't pay his rent leaves in the middle of the night to hole up in the old family shack. This financial pressure also hits hard in 'Milk Teeth' by Isabella Rona where a mum struggling to feed her family is forced to make a heartbreaking choice.

'Tidelines' by Glyn Matthew, inspired by Turner's *Helvoetsluys*, is set in a bleak grey landscape where the lolling red tongue of the killer sheep dog is the only touch of colour. As a counterpoint, 'The Shallows' by Poppy White creates a magnificent underwater seascape which is explored by the forgetful but unforgettable main character Jo.

The next section, *Images*, is about the art of light and shadow. Imagine an eightball on a table, lit by a strong lamp. There are variations of light, shadow and reflection across its surface and on the table too. Artists categorise these variations into a value scale—a palette from white to black with shades of grey in between. For the writer, the challenge is to decide how much light and how much shade is needed to shape their narrative. *Images* is filled with spectacular visual writing and captures moments in time, place and history that will stay with you.

Pleasure and Pain then sweeps out all that is hidden from under the carpet and explores our desires and fears. It brings into the spotlight genuine experiences of abuse, pain, loss and loneliness and it celebrates life, love, dancing and making social connections. Darkness can destroy everything in its path, yet it can also provide shade, shelter and peace.

Moonlight contemplates the vastness of space, life on the moon and a distant future world. Each piece in this collection makes us think about space, and our relationship with it, in a different way.

Electric Lights, Smoke and Mirrors is a collection of stories about the light and shadow in all of us. These stories are about the everyday life that we live indoors, at home, at the shopping centre. As we dance towards the light, craving its warmth and illumination, we can be dazzled by smoke and mirrors and lose ourselves along the way—or we can be consumed and destroyed by the shadows. Life is full of joy, turmoil and beauty. We are all made up of light and shadow.

By paring things back to black, white and shades of grey there is a sense of gravitas, of capturing a moment in time and space, and of keen observation. *Dawn to Dusk* adds the complexity and beauty of colour and reflection. This final chapter explores our connection to the land through strong characters, evocative landscapes and the passage of time.

ABOUT MINDS SHINE BRIGHT

Minds Shine Bright is an arts business that encourages and supports writers, based in Melbourne, Australia. It was founded in 2021 by Amanda Scotney. We run an international creative writing competition each year and publish books. Our aim is to raise the profile of our published writers and to ensure that every published author is paid. We work with writers, book partners and the reading community to spread the appreciation of anthologies far and wide and to build our readership. This takes time, effort, experimentation and ongoing collaboration and is a joy.

Almost 500 entries were submitted between September 2023 and March 2024. During this time there was an increase in international geopolitical tensions and wars, advances in generative artificial intelligence, and the costs of living rose steeply across the globe.[1]

The competition was blind-judged and assessed against key criteria for literary merit. I was joined on the panel by fellow judge and Melbourne based poet and psychiatrist, Jennifer Harrison, whose wisdom, judgment and expertise in the elements of poetry and the written word added great value. As a result of much re-reading, thought and discussion, forty-three writers were shortlisted for publication in *Light and Shadow*.

Light and Shadow provides an evocative reading experience from beginning to end, and the opportunity to discover exciting new talent. You can find out more about the contributing writers and poets in the *About the Writers* chapter at the end of this book. If you enjoyed reading *Light and Shadow* and are interested in becoming an advanced copy reader for future anthologies, please contact us at **writing@mindsshinebright.com**.

---

[1] The cost of living crisis was reported in many reputable economic and news sources across the globe including the IMF Cost of Living Crisis 2023 Report and the RBA Statements on Monetary Policy 2023 & 2024.

1
TOP
ELEVEN

FIRST PRIZE

ISI UNIKOWSKI

CANBERRA, ACT, AUSTRALIA

Isi Unikowski is a Canberran poet. His collections Kintsugi *(2022) and* Re:Vision *(2025) are published by Puncher & Wattman books.*

BRIGHT SQUARE OF MORNING

Leaving Melbourne, the highway curves slowly past
estates
        shoaling into paddocks and foothills,
as if half-inclined to take one last look back
        at the hazy city.
If you leave early enough,
            just at that bend,
        in a line to the distance the road would have
followed if it hadn't turned away,

your eye will be drawn to the side of a large shed
        shining in the dawn; so radiant
that this blank, yellow square is its own light source,
        as if the very point
from which the morning is unfurling.

As the day's distances begin
        and the dozing passengers give you time to think
about another set of appointments kept, opportunities
missed,
        this shape offers just enough distraction

to blunt that retinue's claim until
                    it falls behind
with the B-double convoys dispersing
               into the fat quarters of the interior.

For a moment held by a line of sight, that immanent light
               seems to offer something more than the kilometres
to come
of dishevelled bottlebrush, cable railings
               squaring the gravel verge
adolescent cliques of skewed gum saplings

the brightness of that wall is like a page
               behind which a torch is shining
               revealing a page's opalescent swash,
a trace of the crush and scrape that brings paper out of
water
               as though something of a sapling's leap toward
the sun is echoed in light's flecks and fibres
as if the writing across its face
               is the least important thing.

SECOND PRIZE

HELEN BOOTH
ANGLESEA, VICTORIA, AUSTRALIA

Helen Booth lives on beautiful Waddawarung country on the Surf Coast in Victoria. Her short stories have won the 2024 Minds Shine Bright Confidence Writing Competition, 2022 Apollo Bay Wordfest and 2018 Odyssey House prizes. She has also had stories shortlisted for the 2023 Rachel Funari, 2021 Sydney Hammond Memorial and 2016 Overland Fair Australia prizes.

THE BRIGHTEST STAR

This story is dedicated to my late partner Alan Bland.

Frank's gloved hands grip the wheel. His eyes fixate on the road, navigating through 3am weirdness. Two stripes of crusty, orange-red street gravel roll towards and under the car and he is powerless in an alien world. The road sucks them forward beneath arms of menacing trees that reach from nowhere. He fiddles with the heater knobs, wishing he was home, under the doona, asleep. Dry heat blasts his face and feet. The windscreen fogs.

'For goodness sakes.' Mon presses the demist button, filling the car with a rush of frigid air.

'Remind me again why we're doing this.' Frank says, eyeing the tall greyish lump of Mon beside him—her misshapen beanie, twists of escaping curls, the bulk of the jacket she'd dragged on over two jumpers.

'You didn't have to come.'

'Course I did. Not letting you go down there on your own.'

'Perfectly capable of looking after myself.'

'Anything could happen… '

A kangaroo leaps from nowhere. Frank hits the brakes; tyres skidding, wheels locking. The roo stares through long lashes at the windscreen, paws poised at chest level, every tan hair on high alert. Frank cuts the headlights and it bounds away.

'See?'

Monica shrugs and bangs on the dashboard. 'Onwards, Frank. Onwards.'

Out of habit, he turns left at the carpark into unfamiliar grey emptiness fringed with tangled shapes of wandering moonahs.

'Not here.' Mon says. 'We're not going for a swim.'

'Where then?'

'Told you before, the Point.'

Frank pulls the car into a U-turn.

Gravel mixes with sand as the path to the Point appears telescoped in the high beam. The tyres churn and slide.

'Here?'

'Perfect.'

Mon strides ahead, the steam of her breath haloed in the miner's light strapped to her head. The odd flash of silver bounces from the camera case she insisted on carrying. Frank trudges after her, head down, the tripod dragging on his shoulder, a bag of accessories—for God only knows what—swings from his hand and bounces against his leg. His body sways from side to side, the overtight strap of his miner's light bites the tops of his cold ears, and the light casts a zig-zagging pattern across zillions of sand granules that surge and sink around his freezing feet. Already, he can feel sand filling the soles of his runners.

The rush and hush of the sea grows louder. Nearer. Its salty chill hits his face. He tastes it on his lips. Smells it lining his nostrils, filling his lungs with its icy depths. The path opens out. He's arrived. But where is Mon? He scans monotone stripes of sand, rock, sea.

'Mon'

'Over here.'

'Where?'

'Here …'

He squints into the night. A dark shape he's mistaken for a rock is waving at him. He lumbers on. Hits wet sand and keeps his eye on the shifting outline of Mon moving across the exposed reef. Fool of a woman. Why on earth has she turned her lamp off? She'll fall into a rockpool, or worse, off the edge and into the sea.

Luckily, she stops. Hands on hips. Even at that dim distance, he picks up the flare of her impatience. He rounds the cove, hugging the rock wall. Something in his periphery, inches from his hip, lets out low growl. Panic zaps his chest. He stops. Turns. Spotlighting a vicious mouth full of yellowed teeth, reeking of rotten fish and fringed with whiskers. The beast growls again, eyes gleaming, and lunges at him. Frank runs. Runs from the rock wall straight into a shallow pool. He trips. Almost falls sideways with the bag and tripod but manages to regain his balance. Heart thumping, he searches for the shape of Mon.

She's laughing that deep husky laugh of hers. He sloshes towards her, shoes and socks soaked. Feet numb with cold.

His light finds her face—the red frames of her glasses, her dancing blue eyes.

'Were you terrorizing Harold?'

'Harold?'

'The seal,' she laughs. 'Apparently he's often here at night.'

'Could've warned me. Bastard almost bit me.'

'Turn your light off.'

'Why?

'Just turn it off.'

Frank reaches up, fumbling through gloves.

Mon tuts and snaps his lamp off, her cold fingers brushing his face. 'Now, look up.'

Frank's been so focused on his feet, on finding Mon, finding his way, avoiding death by seal and death by sea, that he never noticed them. Stars. Millions of them. A mass of sparkling whites, pale yellows, swirling pastels of the lightest pinks, violets and even blues. Precious gemstones, some shining brighter than others, floating across the vast sky and trailing off to the east and west.

'There's no moon.'

'Exactly. That's why we're here. I've been following the weather apps. Waiting for the perfect winter night—low tide, no moon, no cloud—just this.' She waves at the glittering sky.

He can't see how a photo could ever do it justice—the expanse, depth, colours, brilliance.

'Come on, quick sticks,' she says. 'Let's get the gear out before the tide turns.' Mon turns her lamp on, assembles the tripod, clicks a lens onto the camera, attaches something else to the top, fiddles with her phone. Frank removes his glove just long enough to flick his lamp on. He finds a flat rock to sit on. Yawns. Hugs himself to keep warm. Shouldn't be too long now. A few snaps and they can go home, and he can get some sleep before his golf day.

Mon hums an annoying little tune over and over while she positions the tripod, peers at the side screen, angles the camera and checks the side screen again.

'Lights off,' she says.

Frank removes his glove for a moment and flicks the switch. A soft, glowing brightness descends from above, from thousands of light-years away. Maybe even before they were born. Mon presses her phone repeatedly. The camera clicks slowly over and over and over.

'Using your phone?'

'Yeah. Remote trigger.'

Frank sighs. 'So many repetitions of the same shot,' he says, voice edged with the petulance of an overtired child. Eyes stinging. Face aching with cold. 'Why?'

'Night photos can have a grainy texture called noise,' she says.

The sea heaves and crashes against the edged of the reef. 'Noise?'

Mon peers in the side screen and presses the remote on her phone. 'I want to capture the clarity of everything we can see, so I need multiple shots of each image, at least thirty. And over time the stars move—so I'll put all those images through the stacker app, line up the layers and bingo, the noise is gone…'

He doesn't get it. 'Isn't that cheating?'

'Nope. It's using technology to give people the gift of all this. And she points at the swirling, shimmering arc above.

Frank wakes to an icy ache in his feet. Has no idea where he is. Pointy bits of rock and barnacles stick into his bum. He blinks up at the Milky Way and stands, knee deep in water. Christ. The tide. 'Mon… Monica…'

'Down here'

'Where?'

'Other side of the rocks.'

He bounds up, scrambles over rocks. At the top he squints into the dark, makes out her shape on flat sand where a thin strip of back beach begins. She's shooting in the opposite direction, all her attention focused on the lighthouse. He wrestles with the glove of his right hand, yanks it off and switches on his light.

'Frank, no light… Please…'

'Mon, the tide's coming in.'

She looks down. 'Oh, good God, so it is …'

The case and bag of equipment sit on a rock beside her. It doesn't take her long to separate the lens and camera, place them in the case, fold the tripod and stuff it into its bag. 'Come on. We've got to get out of here.'

Frank shoulders the tripod, picks up the case and bag. Waves are lapping across the cove. Which way?'

'Always pays to have an escape route,' Mon says. 'This way. Up the beach and over the dunes.'

She dashes off and Frank follows on the heels of her yellow gumboots. She's immune to the rolling surf but every time a wave lands, Frank is calf-deep in freezing brine and struggling with his load.

'Here, give me those,' she says, grabbing the bag and case. 'Now run.'

They huff and puff to the bottom of wooden steps leading over the dunes.

'That was a little close for comfort,' Mon says, gathering her breath and laughing.

'Not funny,' Frank says, wet jeans clinging to his legs.' He mounts the steps, thinking only of a hot shower and bed.

'Never mind,' Mon says from behind. 'When we get home, I'll make us a nice mug of hot chocolate.'

The next night, they retire early. Frank needs to sleep off the worst game of golf he's ever played. His golf buddies thought he and Mon were crazy taking photos at the Point in the middle of the night.

'You know how cold it was last night? 'Keith asked, offering Frank a slice of fruit cake his wife made. 'Three degrees. Three bloody degrees.'

Frank closes his eyes and relaxes into his pillow, wishing Mon would join the Country Women's Association and bake cakes instead of pursuing this ridiculous photography caper.

Raucous chimes rouse Frank. He rolls over, bleary-eyed. Mon's sitting beside him, swiping her phone. 'Damn. Go off, you stupid thing.' she whispers.

'What are you doing?'

'Trying to turn off the alarm so it doesn't wake you.'

'Bit late.'

'Thought I'd go to the Point again… take a few more shots… for the exhibition.'

'What exhibition?'

'Look, it's just a small group exhibition at the local gallery… in three weeks and I just want to get some different perspectives and a panorama.'

'Surely you got enough last night.'

'You don't have to come.'

He's already out of bed, shivering and looking for clothes. 'You're not going down there by yourself.'

For the next two nights, they go. Mucking about in early morning single digit temperatures.

The first night, from a safe distance, they shine their lights and sing out, 'Hello, Harold.' They set up on the exposed reef, ready to begin shooting when a wind rises from nowhere, whipping up ragged dark clouds that snuff out the starlight and turning spots of rain into an almighty downpour.

The second night, Frank wears gumboots, an extra jumper, two beanies and a rain jacket. He marvels at the sky, so clear and bright, and welcomes the sharpness of cold air in his lungs and on his face.

Mon takes multiple shots for her panorama, telling Frank how she'll stack each section of layered images, then stitch them together.

'Last section,' she says. 'Frank, I need you up there.'

'Where?'

'On that large rock formation that backs onto the ocean. See? The one in the middle with that indented ledge on top.'

'Am I in it'?

'Yes. And me—after I frame it.'

Frank picks his way across to the edge of the reef, past the first rock formation. The middle one is higher than it seemed from a distance. He removes his gloves, jams them in his pocket and climbs the rock like an oversized two-legged crab; bending low, finding footings and finger holds, side winding till he's up, balancing, legs shaking, toes inside his gumboots gripping the rough surface. He glances over his shoulder at the sound of crashing waves.

'Little more to the left,' Mon yells.

Frank sidles across.

'Perfect. Here I come.' She leaves the camera on the tripod and bounds across the reef, her miner's light picking out crags, rockpools, the slippery sheen of seaweed.

She climbs the rock with ease, like she's done it before. 'Shove over,' she laughs. 'Gosh, this is beautiful, isn't it, Frank? You can scatter my ashes here.'

'Don't be ridiculous.'

'No, I'm serious.'

Frank refuses to think about that.

'Lights out,' Mon says.

Soft luminescence descends. They are suspended between pitch-black sea and sparkling sky.

'So, what now?'

Mon takes her phone from her pocket. 'I'll press the remote, we pose, count five and snap.'

'Okay.'

'Ready?' She presses the trigger. 'Five.' Shoves the phone in her pocket. 'Four.' Grabs Frank's hand. 'Three.' Waves.

Frank smiles.

'Two.'

He half raises his arm and his foot slips.

'One.' Mon hauls him back.

Snap. It's done. Frank's legs are shaking. He can't look down. 'Can we go now?'

'Not quite. Remember, layers, Frank, layers. Only twenty-nine shots to go.'

A crowd has gathered for the exhibition opening. Everyone's brought a plate to share. The table's centre piece is a tripled-tiered flourless chocolate cake Keith's wife Elaine has baked. It's sprinkled with icing sugar and adorned with berries. Mon chats to Elaine and rips open a packet of chocolate-coated biscuits. No matter how she arranges them on the paper plate, they'll never be as appealing as Elaine's chocolate cake.

Frank takes a fluted glass of sparkling wine from the end of the table and weaves through the crowd to the white walls where photographs of varying sizes hang. Glowing pink and orange sunrises, colours reflecting on sea and wet sand. Bright cascading waterfalls flow through brooding rain forests. Dark, pearly capped seas merge into stormy skies pierced with jagged forks of yellow lightning. They're all good, but none as breathtaking as Mon's massive panorama.

It dominates one wall. Frank stands before it, lost in hints of red cliffs, faint shimmers of indigo sea, inky sky lit with millions of stars. A mass of sparkling whites, pale yellows, swirling pastels of the lightest pinks, violets and pale blues. And there, to the south, the middle rock bearing two tiny figures silhouetted against a three-dimensional sky filled with precious floating gemstones that trail off to the east and west. Mon's left hand holds his, her right hand raised in the air. His legs are wide apart, right arm half raised. The pair of them. Tiny dots in the universe. Their small and sometimes mismatched lives layered and stitched together in this rare moment. No amount of flourless chocolate cake could ever compare to this.

'What do you think?' Mon asks, startling him as she wraps her arm around his shoulder.

'Amazing… unbelievable…'

''Tis, isn't it?… Hey, I've sold five others. One, twice.'

'Twice?'

'Yes—easier enough to print and frame another copy.'

Elaine and Frank appear beside them. 'Gosh, we'd love to buy this one,' Elaine says.

Mon puts on her exaggerated upside-down smiley face. 'Oh sorry, Elaine— you can have any of the others, but this one's not for sale.'

They move off to study Mon's next offering and Frank leans into the warmth of her embrace.

So, can you find the brightest star?

He scans the image. There are so many bright stars…

'Oh, come on, Frank…'

'Um…'

'Look, it's this one,' she says, her finger landing on the tiny silhouette of him.

The artwork described in this story was inspired by the photography of Craig Crosthwaite from SeeSea Images.

THIRD PRIZE

EDIE REDWINE
MILWAUKEE, WISCONSIN, USA

Edie Redwine is a 24-year-old Ojibwe Two-Spirit person living in Milwaukee, Wisconsin, U.S.A. They work in social services and have recently rekindled their childhood love of storytelling. Edie hopes to connect with the writing world through queer and Indigenous imagination.

ROOTS

Zhingobiiwaatigookwe indizhinikaaz. My name is Pine Tree Woman. *Indanishinaabem megwaa-niboyaan.* I say it in Ojibwe as I die. I wake up to the green and blue shadows of the forest. I'm lying on my back on the forest floor. The ground is sharp with frost and my body is rigid against it. My heart beats soft and fast as the mist of my breath swirls upwards. I look up at the moon. The sky is a deep black wound in the conifer needle canopy. I hear a rasping gurgle below me, like a shallow murky river trying to breathe. It keeps running, whistling with my exhales. I am cold, and I don't know how long I've been imprinting on the mud. In the curve of my neck, a vicious pain is beginning to bloom up. The pain flowers with blinding heat. My body is naked and slick with mud, and a burning warmth is dribbling down my neck. It pools in my chest and under my cold back. I try to call out. The only sound the trees hear is a bubbling rasp. I put my hand to my neck, and against the moon my hand is wet with blood from the touch. I try to yell again. The only sound in the forest is blood sputtering from the straining gash in my throat. I go quiet, pressing my hands to my collarbones. My blood flows, my breath still bubbles through it. I push myself to my knees with shaking hands. The bloody earth and tall pines rock and spin. I tangle my hands in rough, sappy branches and pull myself to my feet. My wrists and ankles are braceleted with deep brown bruises. I step up the rocks and twigs. My vision is clear in the moonlit dark. The forest grows taller. The sky grows closer. A torn shirt hangs from a low, barren branch. My eyes meet a hunting knife resting against tree roots. The roots are old and wizened. The knife is young and bright. I know it is my blood that is dried to the blade. The frozen ache in my limbs meets a harsh twilight wind. I hear sleep telling me to come closer. I know that if I answer, my body is never leaving the forest. Perpetual spring ice and the scent of fir balsam and fresh cuts will be my final resting place. I walk forward. Stinging plants and burrs follow my bare feet. The trees blanket my trail with darkness. I am alone. The rasping blood gurgle of my breathing follows me. The forest is silent. I rip into the evergreen woods with scratched fingers. Faces of forest spirits blink at me through the darkness. *I'm alive*, I speak in blood and air. I press my fingers into the warm wound on my neck. I feel the shredded vocal cords against soft tissue. *I'm alive*, I speak again. My words are a hoarse, blood soaked breath. The spirits follow. I come into a burned ashy clearing. The moon is the size of a mountain on the horizon. The opening brings cold air and emptiness. I step on splintering charred wood and walk into the ribcage of the woods. The forest holds me with long, wrinkled fingers. She is keeping me safe within herself. The forest spirit will bury me softly. The highway, the city, fall further into nowhere. I can only see the moon. It is quilted white fabric against the empty sky. I walk. I push against tangling branches and felled logs. Acorn drums and river stone chimes sound in the distance. They beat against each step I take. Curious ghosts scratch my back and trip between my legs. I can feel myself dying. I can feel the eyes of good and bad spirits. And I cannot scream. I throw myself forward. My arms stretch out into darkness and feel dying ancestors touching back. I scream with the muscles in my face. I scream with a silent mouth open wide and spitting blood. I hear a chant following behind me, made of birds and frogs and women and fruit. And my body is heavy. Tears blur my eyes with burning salt. I push myself from tree to tree, and the hours are draining from my neck. And suddenly, the road is close. A rumbling sound and a flash of light flicker through the trees. I press myself forward. My body is slow. My legs stilt like a baby deer. But I walk. I feel myself tugged back. My hair is held by unborn descendants and undead grandparents, and I walk. My blood has poured down the front of my body like a red dress. I walk until my toes hit gravel and I am staring down an empty road. I tear my hair and limbs out of the forest brush and suddenly everything is silent. The spirits, the ghosts, the animals, the ancestors, the insects, my breath, have all gone still as I take a step onto the road and stare down the dark path. I hold the silence and stand at the edge of the road. The moon is behind me and the road is smooth underneath me. Two white lights approach, running towards me. The car is a shiny black, and as it comes close, I step into the center of the road and raise my arms. *I'm alive. I'm alive.* I can see the shadowed faces of the couple driving, coming for me. I watch the wife's red lipstick as they approach and do not slow. And I watch the red, smiling tail lights as the car keeps driving past me. My arms stay raised as the car fades from view. All I can do is listen to my breath spurt through the hole in my neck. I am dying. I look across the road. Two eyes open in the dark space between two trees.

When I was 12 years old, I went to my first ceremony. It was at a small lodge on the edge of my mom's reservation. I remember cutting off all my hair in the back of the van on the drive up. I had jagged bangs across my forehead and a cowlick on the back of my neck. When my mom poured all my siblings out of the van, I came out last. My mom smacked me upside the head and left it at that. At the ceremony circle, I remember the big center fire with a serious looking boy tending it, and the long medicine pipe that the adults fuddled about passing to the younger kids. But before long, dread met cramps in my stomach. I realized that gooey brown blood was staining through my summer shorts. The serious boy noticed first and walked me out of the circle. He was a few years older than me and had pretty eyes and a nose that had been broken too many times.

"You have to go away until the ceremony's over, or you'll mess up the spirits," he said. My ears got hot with rage. I kicked the dirt and ran off. I wandered into a wooded patch far out from the lodge and crouched on a soggy decaying log. I rocked back and forth to soothe my stomach and my fuming head. I hated long drives. I hated the seriousness of ceremony. I hated grouchy elders and fussy little cousins. I hated the spirits for embarrassing me. But most of all, I hated that it was all chosen for me before I had even been born. I sat for a long while, blood staining my seat. Boredom rumbles were setting in when I noticed a pair of small black tendrils poking out of a hole in the log. I leaned in closely and watched a fat black millipede slowly unfurl from inside the rotting wood. It stuck out its head and fluttered its insect legs in the air. I grabbed it with a quick fist, but shuddered and dropped it after feeling its squishy body and frantic army of legs. It hurried along through the brush, and I jumped over the log after it. I crawled through the weeds watching for the small scurrying shadow. I kicked off both my sandals as I followed behind it on all fours like a teenage fox. I suddenly spotted a peaking long antenna coming out from the grass and lunged for it. The millipede sensed me and fled under a thick, old tree root as my cupped hands hit the dirt. I shimmied forward on my stomach and put my hand deep inside the creepy hole under the tree. My eyes followed the winding roots, and I realized that they formed an arch big enough for me to crawl under, like a secret passage into the underbelly of the tree. I flipped onto my back and stared up at the wise old tree. It was a fir tree with a trunk as wide as my family's van, and low hanging branches formed an endless sacred tent dotted with baby pinecones. I slowly got onto my knees and peaked my head under the roots-cave. It was dark, and as open as a secret treehouse. As my eyes adjusted, I could see scattering insects and thought I could almost see the swaying tails of small animals along the walls and corridors. I moved inside with careful hands and bruised knees. The mulch beneath the tree was soft and cool. The cavern smelled like fresh soil and pine sap, and the light from outside disappeared as I wove my way inside. Everything was suddenly still inside the tree. My stomach cramps turned dull and achy, and pine twigs and dead grass stuck to my palms. I reached the center of the roots, where two stood like columns to a doorway. Beyond the opening was dark and quiet. My breathing felt loud, and I could feel a low vibration across the dirt.

"Hello?" I whispered, hoping for no response. The movement stopped. In the dark space between root columns, two eyes opened—one after the other, like a toad. The eyes glowed in the darkness, wet with slime and tears. They were looking at me tenderly. The eyes were wolflike but had the gaze of a prey animal. We stared into each other's eyes unmoving. I could feel a warm breath coming from a face I could not see in the darkness, and it smelled like the steam from a pot of wild rice. Slowly, gently, the spirit reached out a hand. It was big, round and calloused, with gray skin and yellow claws. It held out its palm with expectant eyes. Shaking and sleepy, I carefully put my small hand in the cushion of the spirit's palm. Its eyes flickered.

Nibimaadiz. My name is Zhingobiiwaatigookwe, and I'm alive. I wake up to sunlight on a white wall. I am in a hospital bed, and it is early morning. The blankets are coarse, and I feel hazy and motionless. It smells like cleaning spray and gauze, but next to me I smell cigarettes, car leather musk and home. I reach my hand out to my mom, and she clasps it somberly. I look at her face up close for the first time in years. She is old and her face is a washed-out brown, with cracks and spots. Her eyes have gone saggy, but behind watery wrinkles her black coffee irises are unchanged. She frowns, just like she always has, and her breath is musty. I feel like a child with her at my bedside. She leans in to hold me and whispers, "Every year I thought you were already dead."

I look at my mother's expression. The furrow of her sparse eyebrows matches the harrowed curve of mine. I feel for the first time that I am looking at my own face—the face of a living ancestor that haunts my bloodstream.

"I didn't think to ask if you survived when I got the call."

I look at her with blank eyes. I remember home, and I remember anger and hunger and dirty carpets. I remember missing aunties and shitty frybread and white schools. And I remember why I left. And I remember that it followed me. There will always be pine needles in my shoes.

"Did the attackers cut all your hair off?" Mom strokes my buzz cut with unkind hands. I shake my head, slowly and almost imperceptibly. My head has been shaved since I was 17. I can feel the fresh bandages around my throat, and I put a protective hand against my chest. The bruise around my wrist has deepened. I am silent and I look away from my mother, towards the window. The sunlight filters through spring budding tree branches onto the hospital courtyard. I met a spirit when I was twelve. It met me when I was shedding blood, shedding a reproductive lining that was cursed with ancestral sorrow. And I met that same spirit decades later, when my blood again stained the forest floor. There is a spirit that knows me better, a forest spirit that sees my lineage and blesses it with an end. I feel accepting and rageful. The IV in my hand is cold, and my mom's cheek is hot against my forehead.

"I thought I would never see you again," mom says. "I raised you and I know you. But I don't want to only hear about you when you die. You were lucky, but I know one day I will lose you. Where did my daughter go?" I feel spirits everywhere. The air has always been filled with them, but I guess you only see them when you are a child and when you are going to die. There was no luck for me in the murderer that trailed me. I wear the sign of prey in my heritage colors. But the forest knows me better. I am her daughter. Something else will stay in my blood, and I see it clearly. I push my mother away gently and look up into her eyes. Where did my mother's daughter go? I don't know if words will come out, if they will tear my throat apart stitch by stitch, but I speak. "She's. In. My. Roots."

FOURTH PRIZE

PAUL DREWITT
KARAMA, NT, AUSTRALIA

Paul Drewitt is the author of 5 novels, including CatWalk, Karinya *and* Street Sweeper. *He lives in Darwin with 'the wife, the kids, the dog and the cat,' and he occasionally wears pants. His latest novels, 'Emus Fly North in Winter' and 'Vince Lombardi' are under consideration for publication in 2025.*

SLITHER OF LIGHT

When I lay awake, in my room at night,
There's a slither of light, at the base of my door.

When someone walks by, the light hides,
In bits and pieces, trampled by footsteps.

Some feet are heavy, slow and awkward,
But then others, are nimble and lively.

I soon fall asleep, with the light in my eyes,
Watching the feet, go back and forth.

Then comes a nightmare, a troll with steel claws,
Walking the sewers, and dragging its feet.

I quickly lose sight, of my bedroom door,
As the troll lays upon me, and whispers my name.

Then comes the pain, from way down below,
Like a kitchen knife, driven into flesh.

I can feel the troll breathing, down the side of my neck,
Slowly at first, then faster it goes.

It wants to survive, gasping for air,
Keeping alive, by feeding on me.

I lift my head, from time to time,
Looking for footsteps, and a slither of light.

But all I can see, is the darkness around me,
And all I can hear, is the breath on my neck.

When I wake up, I look at the door,
And the slither of light, has returned once again.

I see people walk by, both awkward and lively,
Talking about things, the way adults do.

TOP ELEVEN

GAYLE BEVERIDGE

WONTHAGGI, VIC, AUSTRALIA

Gayle Beveridge is a past winner of the Boroondara Literary Awards and The Margaret Hazzard Short Story Award. Her work has appeared in anthologies including Storm, Award Winning Australian Writing, Sparx, Transformations, The Umbrella's Shade, *and* Mosaic. *Gayle is a retired accountant living on Australia's beautiful Bass Coast and divides her time between writing, photography, bird watching and walks in the bush.*

CASH ONLY

The corrugated iron of the family fishing shack was already riddled with rust holes by the time I inherited it. I'm expecting it to be worse now. When I open the door to check inside, the sun is setting low over the lake. It skims across the surface, makes its way through those rust-ragged gaps, and paints the dirt floor polka-dot yellow. I'm not worried about the roof. It doesn't rain much here anyway, and I reckon the layer of pine needles up there is at least four inches thick. 'She'll be right.'

I'm the third-generation to own the shack. You'd think there'd be some pride attached to that, but the land isn't mine. It never was, and the shack is jerry-built from scrap. My family were never land owners. When I was young, we moved from rental to rental, sometimes in the dead of night. Nothing's changed. I left my renter last night, my first solo midnight flit. My mood was dark. This was no childhood adventure, not like it used to be. I never imagined I would come to this, but I blinked and when I opened my eyes, I was already in this space. Shame and self-loathing sat on my shoulders and my knees buckled as if I was toting a box of bricks.

I'd packed my clothes into green shopping bags worn floppy from overuse. Jeans in one. T-shirts in another. Underwear, then shoes. I have a jumper—Mum knitted it years ago—and a couple of hoodies. I'll need them later when the weather turns. In winter, the wind sucks the cold from the lake and throws it at the shack until it sets it to rattling. Something spooked me as I carried the bags to the car. A noise... A flicker... A movement... I froze, then turned 360, peering into the night; there was nothing there. Nothing but the shadows of the life I'd screwed up. I packed my laptop; didn't know where I'd get it charged when the battery was done. Same for my phone; I'd have to be careful to use that sparingly. I only had one cardboard box. It was my kitchen now—a saucepan, a frypan, a mug, a plate, a bowl, some cutlery. My fishing gear was a must; it was my meal ticket. I rolled my sheets and doona straight off the bed and put them and my pillow and towels on the righthand side of the boot. I wanted everything out of sight; didn't want people to think I was living in my car, even if I was.

My landlord is hundreds of kilometres away now and yet he isn't... he's here, strutting and grumbling in my head. He must have been seriously pissed when he realised I'd skipped. Has he rung? I've had my phone turned off all day. I reach for it, but leave it in my pocket. Thing is, he's not a bad bloke. I was renting the granny flat in his backyard. We'd got to know each other, even had a beer or two together. For the last couple of months, I've been holding him off, lying about still having a job. I can't pay him, and I can't face him either. 'I'm sorry mate.'

The light is disappearing, and I rush to get my bedding set up on the old canvas stretcher, surprised it hasn't rotted. At least I hope it hasn't. 'I'll find out soon enough.' I spent what little cash I had in the same roadhouse where Dad and I used to stop. The town is over ten klicks back, but I can see its glow on the horizon as I have a late dinner - a bowl of cereal and long-life milk. That'll be breakfast too. It was all I could afford after I topped up with petrol. The hot meat pie in the bain-marie looked appealing, but it cost more, and I needed a toilet roll. Besides, that pie would only have done one meal. Never mind, I'll go fishing tomorrow. I don't have a licence but that's the least of my worries.

Washing in the early morning waters of the lake is bracing, but not in a good way. 'I'm not looking forward to winter.' Sleep was hard to come by last night. I was done with my problems for the day, but my mind had other ideas. The thoughts came unbidden. They were protestors waving signs painted with angry red letters; they shouted, each demanding attention, and I was outnumbered. I was dizzy from the need for sleep, foggy headed and lead footed. Bed beckoned, but I shut the door on it. I'd seen a staff wanted sign in the window as I'd left the roadhouse last night.

The sign is disappointing in daylight; faded ink on yellowed paper curled at the edges. Perhaps they'd forgotten to take it down. Still, nothing ventured, nothing gained. That's what Mum always said; not that it did her any good. There's nobody at the counter, so I strike the bell and jerk in surprise as that sound jumps around the walls. I've belted it too hard, nearly knocked it to the floor. They might think I'm angry and that won't do. I'll come back tomorrow... maybe.

'Help you with something?' He came out from the back, knotting the ties on a greying apron.

'Um, I saw the staff wanted sign in the window.' I point to it and then drop my finger, realising he'd know bloody well where it is.

He whistles, sharp, shrill, and piercing, and yells even louder. 'Merv, bloke here about the job!'

Merv is a big man, well-fed, his T-shirt strains and stretches. He has white-haired gorilla arms with faded hints of old tattoos. He's bald, but his bushy salt-and-pepper beard amply compensates for that shortcoming. 'It's a mixed job, waiter, counter sales, stocking shelves, cleaning,' he says. 'What's your experience in hospitality?'

'I'm, um, a hard worker... good at taking instruction... a fast learner.'

He picks up a tea-towel and runs it over the counter where my sloppy words had spilled. 'No experience then. What were you working at, son?'

I feel my shoulders slump. They drag on me like they're hinged with rusty bolts. 'I was a brickies labourer,' I say, my words just a puff.

'No need to whisper, no shame in honest work.' He puts both hands on the counter and leans forward. 'Here's the deal,' he says. 'We serve lunch from twelve to two and dinner from five to eight. Not a minute before, not a minute after. Most of our customers are truckers and loggers, all opinionated blokes with big egos. You'll be working the afternoon shift; noon to nine, Thursday to Tuesday. I don't give a rat's arse for bookwork and I won't be doing any. I pay cash, $150 a day. Don't talk to me about award wages; if you don't like the money don't take the job. Friday is payday. Piss me off and you're out. Piss Rory off,' he points towards the back, 'and you're out. Piss the customers off, and you're out. I'll give you a two-day trial. If you don't work out, you don't get paid. Take it or leave it.'

'I'll take it,' I say, letting no pause settle. I'm probably a bit eager, but hey, I'm living in a tin shed, and it's Thursday. If this works out, I'll get three hundred dollars tomorrow.

'Right then,' Merv reaches out and we shake on it. 'Come back at eleven and I'll show you the ropes before the lunch rush.'

The loggers come en masse for lunch. They clump in on dusty boots and crowd the counter. Several of them order, all talking at once, and right away I don't know who I should serve first. Merv sidles up. 'Remember,' he says, loud enough for them to hear, 'they order at the counter and the menu is the menu— no variations. And it's cash only. There's the ATM in the corner if they need it.' They laugh.

An older bloke, with wiry verandah-eyebrows and dirt-encrusted fingernails, slaps a twenty on the counter. 'I'll have the steak and chips and salad, and you can keep the lettuce, coz I wasn't brought up to be a rabbit.' More laughter. He's right, he's no rabbit, he's a cat and I'm the mouse he's tormenting before the kill.

'You'll have the salad as it comes, and it's twenty-three dollars.' I raise myself to full height, stare into his eyes, and I don't touch his twenty until he puts the rest of the money down. I'm already calling 'next' as I hand him his number. I'm sweating and hoping they don't notice.

Twice this afternoon, I have to get help with the register. It doesn't have a barcode reader, and I can't always find the right keys for the products. Merv clears it and puts it through himself. He says nothing and that clobbers my confidence more than his words would. I mess up one of the orders at dinner time and it goes back to the kitchen, wasted. Rory scrapes the meal into the bin. 'You just blew the profit on the next three meals,' he says.

Most of the dinner crowd are truckers. Their rigs are parked up for the night. The only one left is the guy who had to wait for his meal to be redone. He stops eating and gives me the evil eye as I clear the next table. I guess I've pissed him off too. That's three for three, so I'm not surprised when Merv calls me. He's sitting at a table in the corner with Rory, and they're both looking at me. I look back and steel myself.

'Come on,' Merv beckons. 'Leave that for a bit. Your dinner's ready.' I see the meals then. Three of them. Chips and rissoles smothered in a thick steaming gravy, just the way Mum used to serve them. Rory's already tucking into his. It looks bloody marvellous. It smells bloody marvellous.

'I don't have the money for it,' I tell Merv, and I say it like it's nothing because my dignity is frayed, and I'm desperately clinging to its last threads.

He laughs. 'Sit your arse down and dig in. Perk of the job. It'll just be what we've got left, but it'll hit the spot.' I'm eating before he finishes the sentence.

It's past nine by the time Rory and I finish up in the kitchen. I'm putting the last of the plates away when Merv comes in. 'Day one down,' he says. 'We'll see how you go tomorrow.'

It's dark when I get back to the shack. I should boil some water; it's not coffee but at least it will be hot. I'm buggered though. I can't be bothered lighting a fire. I close the door and power up my phone because I need the torch until I get into bed. Three missed calls. Three text messages. Damn. All from Gavin, my landlord. Damn. I check the texts.

'What's going on with you? You've been weird for weeks.' That was yesterday afternoon. I'd promised him the back rent and given him an empty flat.

'At the very least mate you owe me an explanation. Call me.' That one at seven this morning. He would have been getting ready for work.

'Where are you? If you won't talk, at least text. Let me know you're all right.' Just over an hour ago.

I strip down to my underwear and crawl into bed. I read the texts again. Twice. It's that last sentence—Let me know you're alright—that's carving me to bits. I can't talk to him though. I've been a bastard. I am a bastard. 'Let me know you're alright.' What am I supposed to do with that? Exhaustion is making everything ache, my legs, my arms, even my fingers. I'm desperate for sleep, but I can't let go of that text. I have to answer.

'I'm sorry I skipped. I can't pay you, but I will one day. It's going to take a while. Can't tell you where I am. Sorry.' My phone's still at 80% charge but I turn it off anyway and slide it under my pillow.

Day two and I'm running on auto at the roadhouse, pushing through the weariness and feeling like a boxer punch-drunk from a head pounding. The loggers come in for lunch and verandah-eyebrows is the first at the counter again. I don't ask what he wants, I just wait. He holds out his hand. 'Reckon we got off to a bad start yesterday,' he says. 'I'm Dave.' We shake; I don't tell him my name. Sometimes I look up and Merv's watching. Sometimes Rory's watching. I make it through. There's just one register muck up today and I get all the orders right, or maybe I don't, but nobody bothers to complain.

There's not a customer in the place when we sit down for dinner tonight. It's lamb chops with mashed potatoes and beetroot salad. Merv makes us all a coffee and I nod my thanks. We eat in silence; they're not big talkers, that much I understand.

'You figured out that Rory and I are partners,' Merv asks, but he doesn't wait for an answer. 'We know this place isn't all that much, but it's ours and we've worked bloody hard for it. We're not looking for trouble, so son, whatever it is you're hiding from, is that going to bring us trouble?'

I shake my head.

'You in strife with the police?' Rory throws it out there, the elephant in the room.

'No. No. I swear. I lost my job, and I couldn't pay my rent, that's all.'

'Why here then? What brought you down here?'

'I inherited a little holiday place from my parents. I'm living there.'

'Alright.' Merv stands. He goes to the register, brings back three hundred dollars and he counts it out. 'We'll clean up,' he says. 'Go home and get a good night's sleep. We don't want you passing out on the job. And son, if there's any trouble, you're out.'

'There won't be trouble.' I drag myself up, my eyes on Rory.

He smiles, 'See you tomorrow, then,' he says.

I sit in the car and for a while I just stare at my money. The registration is due next month; I'll have enough to pay for it by then. One day I'll have enough to pay Gavin what I owe, then I'll be square again. It'll all work out as long as I can stay in the shack. I know I'm not supposed to be living there. That's not a worry for today though. Today, Merv and Rory have shone some light into my life, and I want to savour that warmth.

TOP ELEVEN

GLYN MATTHEWS

CONGLETON, CHESHIRE, GREAT BRITAIN

Glyn Matthews is an escaped teacher of English, Art and Drama from the United Kingdom, for many years a professional artist/poet, gradually evolving into a writer of prose with a passion for shorter written forms. Although he writes for adults, he listens to the child that resides inside himself and writes to wake the child that hides in others. His short stories have won or been placed in various competitions in UK, US and Australia.

TIDELINES

The day dawned flat and grey. Naked mudflats lay under a pancake of cloud. Devoid of shape and distance, the eye was robbed of perspective—a warning not to take the shifting mud for granted. Despite the calm, it was a day to mend nets rather than cast them.

Eventually a blade of silver light scratched a line along the horizon and Grandmother hung washing out, hopefully. But shirts hung limp, inverted in surrender.

Grandfather crossed the yard toward the Land Rover and gestured me on board. 'Come on, boy' he called, as if he didn't know my name. As if I was a dog. I climbed in and braced myself and we headed south along the unmade track toward the shifting spit of land that marked the limit of my world.

Open-topped, we drove beside the flats, lurching through puddles that drank the light. The ancient vehicle was the same colour as the track, the mud, the leaden sky. Stretching into the distance, mirror pools abandoned by the tide were pocked with birds and their inversions. Had we stopped and killed the engine, we would have heard the distant cries of mewling waders and chiding gulls. On any other day, the wind might serenade my parents' fading ghosts, snatched and drowned. But that day, just the vehicle's motion stirred dead air.

Suffocated wrecks of skiffs and dinghies with ruined prows emerged from the cloying surface. Abandoned graves with names obscured, 'Bay Dreamer' and 'Shore Thing' gone to hell along with 'Salty Dog' and 'Sea Ya Later'. Weeds, like rotten flesh, hung from carcasses. I scanned each long forgotten pleasure craft and, more slowly, the working boats, searching for my parents' blackened bones.

On the eastern rim, a hidden lesion in the clouds let hard light kiss the distant waves, cold and unforgiving. Shading my eyes, I traced a northbound tanker, crawling across the horizon, like a cut-out target at a sideshow—a black silhouette on shimmering silver, a shadow balanced on the knife edge of the world.

I wondered if Grandfather ever thought to scan the flats as I did. His ragged eyes, bleached and rimmed with nicotine, peered from below his cap's slick brim, his hard mouth clamped upon an unlit dimp. I asked him why he didn't light it, and he told me, without turning, it was there to remind him to keep his mouth shut.

On the elbow of his jacket, a leather patch flapped like an injured bird and his frayed cuff sent random threads to mingle with the hairs sprouting from his wrist. His knuckles showed hard white against the worn black of the steering wheel and his calloused hands were ingrained with dirt that no amount of scrubbing could remove. His whorled fingertips aped ancient fossils trapped in stone.

I glanced across and wondered if he was ever born or had he simply grown from ribs of wrecks and nameless flotsam rejected by the stinking tide? One day, perhaps, his skin will split and let his skeleton escape and no one will feel obliged to tend his grave. Not even my grandmother. Perhaps, especially not her.

We were on our way to Mrs Flynn's, my grandfather's cousin, I believe, though never any kind of aunt to me. In fact, I never knew her first name or even thought to ask. She remained a stranger to me. She kept a rundown farm by the track that petered out into the curling slug of the estuary. There she grieved her husband's death, drowning in its bitter aftertaste. Grief is not always a cake for sharing. I know. My own slice was hidden well enough.

Although there was little comfort there, Grandfather called upon her from time to time. What duty drove him I could only guess. Perhaps my presence excused him from a longer stay and so, perhaps, I served a purpose.

Sometimes, I stayed in the car, my eyes half closed, listening to curlews high above the sliding estuary. Other times, I walked until my boots oozed in the no-man's-land unclaimed by sea or shore. There I stood and let my toecaps be kissed by tiny overlapping waves, lace fringed like floating doilies. I watched my footprints slowly fill, creating pools for tiny twitching things.

Standing on the shoreline, amongst empty razor-clams and lugworm casts, fed my inner need for melancholy. The sucking mud that held my shoes also sucked the living shadow of my soul and drew me ever out to sea. I had to force my eyes to look above the waves and search for light instead of empty graves.

On the estuary's far shore, Scots pine conferred in groups, their needles stitched randomly with shabby crows. Above a low tide calm, their quarrelling seemed unnaturally close. Between the trees, a church tower pointed to the sky, dark and ancient. I imagined chimes rolling out across the water, calling ghosts of mariners to the shelter of her stone skirts.

In the last mile or so before we reached Mrs Flynn's, I leant against the rattling door and let my gaze settle, once again, upon the mudflats' endless grey, the slipstream just enough to leach a tear.

It was then I saw the dog, huge and black, running alongside, its red tongue lolling in a flash of livid colour stolen from a Turner foreground. It seemed intent on keeping pace. In the open vehicle I felt exposed. Bounding closer, it seemed about to leap, trapping my voice, even as I tried to cry a warning. But then it veered away to scatter feeding waders from a nearby pool. Wings clawed at flaccid air, fighting gravity, as the dog leapt into the water, creating a fountain of spray. I turned to Grandfather, but he was oblivious, his eyes fixed upon the rutted track ahead.

I looked back, scanning the flats, my hand shading my eyes searching for the beast against the light, afraid it would return. But it had vanished from the landscape, banished to the shadows as if it had never been, and I kept my silence.

Arriving at the farm, we were greeted by the sight of a police pickup slewed across the yard, blue light bouncing off the peeling whitewashed wall. Mrs Flynn, chilblained and apron clad, with wayward hair, was pointing out across the marram grass to where blobs of sheep lay dotted, their bloody throats ripped out. As far as I could tell, none were left alive. The officer finished making notes and gave my grandfather a passing nod. He mouthed into his radio and then departed, the pickup splashing onto the track. Grandfather spat upon the gravel and rolled a cigarette while raucous crows descended to pluck out sightless eyes. Mrs Flynn waved her arms briefly in futile protest, but there was nothing to be done but phone Howlett and ask him to bring his truck and a couple of his lads to salvage the corpses. Grandfather told me to stay in the car. From there I watched as more crows landed, black bandits, joined by flapping gulls as greedy and raucous as any corvid. Grey and yellow beaks stabbed into open wounds.

We waited until Howlett and his lads arrived. They dragged the bodies with grappling hooks into the yard before hoisting them on board. Howlett dispatched a couple that were still alive, one already devoid of eyes. The smell of blood and faeces hung in the slack air and Grandfather rolled another cigarette. He smoked and talked for a while with Mrs Flynn in the doorway of the farm, their voices drowned by frenzied birds and swearing men. Casting his fag aside he waved briefly to Howlett before returning to the Land Rover.

Neither of us spoke as we drove back, and the light was fading as we trudged across the yard. Inside, I shrugged off my boots and washed at the stone sink, gasping with the shock of cold water on my fevered cheeks. I laid the table, waiting in vain for hunger to tap me on the shoulder. Before the meal, I stood by the window gazing out beyond the empty washing line, watching a lone gull on the drystone wall, something squirming in its beak. Using one of the larger stones as a butcher's slab, it began stabbing at an orange crab, ripping its legs off one by one.

The last gyrations of the stricken crab still behind my eyes, I sat at the table while Grandmother slopped tasteless shepherd's pie on plates which spread like shifting mudflats, more easily consumed with spoons. We spoke a toneless grace and asked God for his mercy, then ate in silence while the rising wind rattled at the window that faced the darkening estuary, heralding the tide's return and bringing in the rain.

I sat and forced the shifting landscape into my protesting mouth, retching quietly on my parents' graves. Outside, in the dusk, the abandoned crab shell glowed faintly. Rain came in waves, drumming at the glass and bouncing off the empty carapace in a vain attempt to bring it back to life.

Later, in the pressing dark, I nursed my tender bones in bed, curled against the slamming of the storm and listened to the slapping night and the sucking of the tide. And as I slipped through the trapdoor to troubled sleep, at the very edge of hearing, I thought I heard the distant baying of a hound.

TOP ELEVEN

POPPY WHITE

HARCOURT, VIC, AUSTRALIA

Poppy White has been writing from a very young age, and in 2024 she won acclaim for several short stories, which were subsequently published in various anthologies. Her writing explores her deep and rich lived experience, as she endeavours to expose the beauty, humour and grief that lies within the fault lines of our human condition. Poppy is represented by literary agent Lou Johnson, at Key People Management and is currently completing her debut novel, Taking Apart Marigold Hart.

THE SHALLOWS

Joe stood and watched vines of refracted light bounce and dance across the pock-holed surface of the shallows. He thought they looked like neural pathways. Travel worn thoughts passing through passages and sparking synapses. Information expressways. Joe's thoughts sometimes strayed from the brightly lit highways, into dark and shaded places. Translucent fish shot through the vines of light in tiny schools and turned about face, surprised by his feet, darting off into obscurity. He bent down and swished salt water around his snorkel and mask. Joe felt his hips and lower back pull, the sting in the arches of his feet. Getting old was a constant series of aches, always shying away from niggles of past injuries. He stood up and stretched his broad shoulders, spattered now with grey hairs, contrasting the deep tan of his wrinkled skin.

This cove was often a sanctuary for lost and forgotten creatures. Joe had come down here once, long ago, and found it teeming with dark stingrays, their curling wings flapping up and splashing awkwardly. They chased one another and came dangerously close to beaching themselves. Did stingrays beach? He wasn't sure. He'd made a mental note to google it later, but a knife had turned deep in his stomach, because he knew he wouldn't remember. Something was wrong. He'd known it that day, watching the stingrays clamber around, fumbling their flat bodies into one another, searching the seafloor for unknown treasure. Joe had watched them for a very long time, until the spattering of rain hardened and drove him from the deserted beach. He never knew if they'd found what they were searching for, but he never saw them again. He still didn't know if stingrays beached.

Joe waded over the moonscape sand toward a rocky outcrop. He sat in a basin of rock and waited. Complete stillness. He knew this was what he must do. And to the patient go the spoils. True patience is an artform. Stopping and clearing away the clutter that bulks up our thoughts and brings our breath short. The constant natter of crowds and the internal monologues that drip into mundane obsolescence. An artform, to sit as a stonefish does, blending and breathing and slowing its heartrate. A heron, poised as a statue in shallow swampland, its long, thin legs unfaltering. And now, his spoils arrived. The bay had forgotten him and frilling out from a crevice in the gritty rock, swam a seahorse. Its brown body mottled and spiky. It motored about upright, fanning its fin, dipping in and out of the weed. He was captivated, then he saw another approaching, with its curled tail and elegant head, held almost coyly away from the first, and they began to circle one another, courting. It was a pompous dressage, and he was bearing witness to this secret waltz. In his mind, he heard his sister Alice whisper, 'Look, Joe, they're dancing. See?' her blue eyes were transfixed. They had once rescued seahorses from their father's fishing net and set them back in this same cove. He looked across to her and was horrified to see Alice's eyes were hollow. She held a dead seahorse up to him. It lay gelatinous and semi-transparent, gruesome in death. And he knew that Alice was dead too. He couldn't forget that.

There was something about the shape of the sea horses' curling tail, the fat belly. What was it about that shape? Then he saw it; he remembered the brain scan. He remembered a doctor turning to him, peering over his glasses that were balanced superiorly, on his nose, 'you see here, Mr. Flannigan? The seahorse shape? The hippocampus.' He pointed at Joe's fate with a blue Bic biro, and he spoke in indifferent, short and fitful sentences. 'Responsible for long term memory formation, and all memory retrieval. Shaped like a seahorse, see?' Tap with the biro. 'Due to the way it's folded in development, yes?' Tap again with the biro. 'Among one of the areas first damaged with Alzheimer's.'

The seahorses continued their dance, but he flinched. Their synchronicity was disturbed. They sensed him and faltered, darted for the safety and camouflage of the chasm. Joe rolled his shoulders and squinted out beyond the cove. The sea pumped and turned, out at the whistling buoy, past the creaming shore break. It was slate grey, and he couldn't tell where the ocean stopped and the cloud began. It all blended into a melancholy brine and suffused his soul with a wariness that felt innate. She was angry today alright, spraying and spitting and breaching the rocky arms that reached out to form the heads of the cove. He pulled on the torso of his wetsuit, familiar like a second skin. He picked up the mesh bag and tied it to his dive belt, then waded into his mother ocean and was welcomed inside her violent belly.

As soon as his head was submerged, he fell into the easy rhythm of his breath. Steady in, slow out. So loud in his ears. Nothing else but him and his breath. The sea pushed and pulled at him, and he submitted to her, allowing himself to drift a little, and then pumping his strong legs towards his goal. Joe felt for the sheath on his waist belt that held his Paua knife. He kicked harder toward the rocky shelf at the entrance of the cove. Joe looked down at the weedy, green sea floor. Like wheat in the wind, like the wheat that, at that moment, was being sown eight hundred and twenty-three kilometres from there, on the farm in Broken Hill. The burn in his legs was good. The lactic acid pulled him away from the shadowy wheat. He focused on his breath. Steady in, slow out.

The light changed so completely down here, in the depths. It bounced around through vines and hidden tracks in the current. Again, he was reminded of his pathways of pruned memory. Joe's trained thoughts ran like an easy freeway through the guts of this cracked, brown country, always running back to Broken Hill. He struggled on through the frothy chop. Down below the weed was getting thicker. It rose long from the ocean floor, reaching for the light. Fish darted between these stretching arms of kelp, hiding in the shadows. Joe imagined lying on the sea floor and peering up through the green and red and bone brown weeds to the vast, violent surface.

His thoughts strayed. They skirted the deep shadows, out of focus, and it scattered his centre. He stopped kicking and floated atop this forest. With his limbs star fished, he focused on the muted light playing through the feathered fronds of weed. It swayed, golden wheat as far as the eye could see, and it beckoned him. Joe heard someone calling. Was she down there? Lost in the soupy sea? No, the wheat. He shook his head. She is always in the wheat. She laughed and ran, and he glimpsed her dress. Forget-me-not blue, zig zagging through the endless lines of bronze, whispering wheat.

'Joe,' she called. 'Joe!' and she poked her face up, laughing.

'Alice!' he caught her. She was happy and tiny.

'Look, Joe,' she squinted and pointed to the burnt evening sky, a murmuration of starlings, a black cloud dancing and flowing like smoke. They were turning and swarming in kinetic alchemy. Inexplicable. Joe sank onto his back, looking longingly up through the corridor of wheat and was bewildered by the birds... or were they fish? Flashing iridescent as they caught the light. Joe turned his head, 'Alice?' the field was empty. The kelp swayed. The swell beat. 'Where was she?'

Joe followed her down that shadowy path. He saw her now. The vivid blue of her dress brought salty bile to his throat. She was climbing a silo. 'No!' he called. She laughed, as though it were a game. 'No!' he called again. The light was faltering. Flickering like a sepia toned, home movie. The buoy was boiling and whistling in the swell. The starlings began to swoop and dive, clouding his view. He swatted at them. Joe couldn't see her anymore. The starlings turned into frantic bubbles. 'Stop!' He screamed. But it came out muffled, strange. There was something in his mouth. The snorkel.

Joe's breath quickened. He blinked rapidly. The swell tossed him, and he couldn't focus. Saltwater leeched into his mask, stinging his eyes. Breathe in, in, in. Quick. The barrel of his snorkel sank below the surface, and he sucked a lungful of burning water. He spat his snorkel. Shook his head. Joe breached from the ocean, only to be smacked hard in the face by a wave. It turned him about, and he summersaulted.

Look for the light. He breached again and coughed. Saltwater spraying from his nose. Joe spluttered and gained his bearings. The grey light through the heavy cloud was stark after the underwater shadow world. He registered the next set of waves bearing down. Joe coughed the remnants from deep in his lungs and took a breath, just in time to duck dive the next wave. Up, breathe, wave, duck. Up, breathe, wave, duck. There were six waves in the set.

When the creamy churning finally settled for a spell, he lay on his back, floating starfished on the surface. He caught his breath, rested his limbs. Joe checked that his Paua knife and mesh sack were still attached at his belt and took a last look at the next set rolling toward him, then dove.

Calm, swaying kelp, with its tangled shadows and impossible depths. He kicked hard then. Joe came back to the surface and breathed, steady in, slow out. He made his way toward the rocky outcrop, the shelf hiding treasure on its curved underbelly. He pushed his burning lungs and reached the porous, cratered rock shelf.

Stay with the light.

Joe extended his hand to touch the rocky surface. The skin of his hand was harbouring tiny bubbles, like minute pearls. It appeared that his hand was not his own. Alien. He took a big breath and dove. Joe's snorkel bubbled as it filled with water. He felt along the underside of the shelf. The abalone clung to the rock fiercely, the way his shadow memories clung to the periphery. Although slowly, one by one, his memories were being pried from their dark moorings and thrust into the light. He took out his Paua knife and began working it between the rock face and the thick shell, until finally, the mollusc submitted, and the creamy brown and yellow flesh was revealed. He shot back to the surface for a breath and then returned to pry another from its stronghold. On his third abalone, he looked at the cluster of shells crowding the rock face and suddenly, he saw her. She was further in, along the cavernous shelf, her face wavering and sinking into the dark, clustered shells. But they weren't shells now. It was sorghum. Her pale face was sinking, drowning. She pleaded.

'No!' Joe called. Then he saw him. His brother, Vern, was holding her down there. He was pulling on her bare legs, refusing to release her. Smirking up at him through the murky depths. Joe got another mouthful of harsh salt water and scrambled to the surface, spluttering and choking. Joe composed himself enough for another dive. His eyes searched along the bumpy shells; their wiry green hairs drifted in the updraft from the yawning chasm. She was gone. So was Vern. Joe made sure his abalone were safely tucked into their mesh bag; he made sure his knife was secure in its sheaf and fled from the dark. He began the steady grind back to shore. Stay with the light. Don't drift.

Joe pulled himself back through the shallows and sat, panting and spent on the wet sand. His abalone sack at his side. He heard a voice in the distance. A man's voice.

'Dad? Dad!' A man was taking the wooden steps that lead to the beach two and three at a time. Bounding. Such athleticism. 'Dad, what the fuck are you doing?'

'That you Vern?' Joe smiled up at him. 'You were a good brother Vern. I'm sorry about Alice.'

'What the fuck, Dad? It's me, Jack.' The man shook his head and looked at him, worry in those deep eyes. 'Dad, you can't just come down here on your own and go swimming anymore. Fuck's sake!' he reached down, and Joe slipped his hand into the man's strong grip. Joe saw the paper wrinkle of his hands. Alien. The man pointed in the direction of the rickety steps.

'Jesus Dad. I leave you for an hour to go to the shops, and you decide to go fucking snorkelling? There's a major swell.'

Joe smiled and held up the abalone, 'got us lunch.'

The man shook his head at him. Smiled despite himself. 'Yeah, I can see that.'

They made their way back to the wooden steps, and as they began their climb, the man stopped Joe again. 'Seriously Dad, you could have got lost in the big drink today. You can't do it anymore. You'll drown mate. Promise me, you won't go out on your own anymore.'

Drown. Joe thought on the word, rolled it over his tongue, then slowly and quietly said, 'Alice drowned.' Then his eyes widened in realisation. 'It was you!' Joe said, pulling away horrified. 'Vern, it was you! I remember now. Swallowed by the soupy sea. I saw her out there. I saw *you* out there.'

'Dad, Alice didn't drown in the sea,' the man shook his head, eyes narrowed and searching.

'The wheat,' Joe whispered, 'the wheat in Broken Hill. She drowned in the silo, Vern. In the sorghum. You pushed her. I saw you.' The man's breath caught in his throat.

'Dad? You saw Vern push your sister? When you were kids? Oh, fuckin' hell Dad.'

Joe burst then, like the banks of the Murray in hundred-year flood, he just welled up and he knew it wasn't Vern. That strong young man pulled Joe in, and Joe grimaced, rigid in grief. He was relieved as the shadowed memory finally pulled free from its mooring and streaked into the light. Joe breathed now. 'Come on mate,' said the man, 'let's get you back, hey? out 'a this wetsuit. I'll make you a cuppa.' The sun broke free from scattering cloud now, bathing them in rich, afternoon light. 'We can cook up these abalone too,' Joe said.

'Sure thing, Dad.'

Joe smiled and closed his eyes, and he saw the veins of scarlet and pink behind his eyelids. Those neural pathways again.

'Stay with the light, Alice,' he whispered.

TOP ELEVEN

SUZANNA FITZPATRICK

ORPINGTON, ENGLAND, UNITED KINGDOM

Suzanna Fitzpatrick (she/her) is a bisexual poet with poems on BBC Radio 4 and widely published in the UK, US, Ireland, Australia and Canada. She was shortlisted for the 2019 Bridport Prize, third in the 2023 Shepton Snowdrops Competition, second in the 2016 Café Writers and 2010 Buxton Competitions and won the 2014 Hamish Canham and the 2024 Newcastle University Chancellor's Prizes. Her pamphlets are Fledglings *(2016), and* Crippled *(due 2025), both with Red Squirrel Press, UK.*

THE SHED

has a glass roof which leaks,
is a stifling hothouse in sun –

no equipment save wooden tables
from the old anatomy school

on which Marie teases apart atoms,
dissecting the undissectible.

This is their space, shared
like their research, the Physics Nobel,

the professorship which passes to her
at Pierre's death. She'll continue alone

accruing breakthroughs, prizes
and high levels of radium

poisoning her bones. She doesn't know;
feels only *joy* in work. Each evening

she pauses before leaving, looks back
at her discoveries, glowing

like faint, fairy lights, smiles,
shuts the door.

Note: The words in italics are Marie Curie's own, taken from her 'Autobiographical Notes' pp. 186–7.

TOP ELEVEN

KEREN HEENAN
MELBOURNE, VIC, AUSTRALIA

Keren Heenan has won a number of Australian short story awards and placed second in the Fish Prize. She was also a winner of the Griffith Review Novella Project 2019. She has been published in Australian journals and anthologies, and in anthologies and online in the US, UK and Ireland.

THE COLOUR OF AIR

Is the air a colour, Mama? he asks.

No, she says.

But I thought I saw it. He looks around as if to point it out to her.

It's only the colour of the things it picks up and moves around, like if there's a wind.

If someone could never see a colour, could you describe it to them? he asks.

She thinks for a while, looking out the window. Well, I don't think so. You can only point it out, like that shirt, or like that flower. If a person is colour blind, they would still see the colour they always see, not the colour others see. Is that what you mean?

No, not really.

When you said you thought you saw the air, she says, maybe it was just the colour you felt at the time. Does it change, this colour you saw? Or is it always the same?

He draws his brows together, pushes his bottom lip out, thoughtful. No. I think it's different. I've seen it silver. And then I think it was blue. The sort of blue that's really pale and shiny so you don't know if you've really seen it, or like, maybe your eyes are... inventing it. It's not blue like anything we can see here, and he moves his hand around the room, towards the window, the trees, the sky, the people and dogs and children walking past. Like, not blue like that boy's shorts, he says, and not blue like the sky, and not that blue, the woman's bag.

You're a clever boy, Archie. Did I tell you that?

Yes, you did, Mama. But I'm not. Not clever like Mason or Amir or Louis. They'd be… even more clever now, he adds.

So are you. You're older now too.

It's different though, he says. It's not just because we're older now. He looks away, out the window, to the trees barely moving, the clouds all puffed up and cottony, back to the tipped-over rubbish bin, the front gate leaning on its broken hinge. Can they come and visit yet? he asks, knowing the answer, so he doesn't look at his mother's face.

She doesn't answer. Reaches out to his hands resting one over the other on the quilt, stops a few centimetres away, her fingers stroking air.

I know, he says, looking at the space between her fingers and his. Thinks he sees a splash of violet flicker, then blue, then nothing.

I'll get your dinner, she says. Then you can have a nap.

He looks at her, thinks, yes, blackness, but he doesn't speak it. Watches her move away, the shimmering whiteness between the door and the doorjamb narrowing as the door quietly closes behind her. His fingers smooth the sheet while his eyes seek out something moving outside, in the garden, on the street, in the air. But all is still and quiet.

His mother returns with his dinner on a tray. She's gone to such trouble; the mashed carrots with honey on top, the vegetable juice in his old Disney Aladdin glass, slices of stewed pear arranged in a circle around three blueberries. He has no appetite, but he cannot tell her. Must push himself up into a sit against the pillow and pick at the food with more energy than that of the tiny bird he feels. A sparrow. Or a wren. Yes, a wren, like the one he saw on a current of pale blue air, lifting off from the fence and flying to the side mirror of a car. Perching there, flitting and turning and preening himself in front of the mirror. But Archie must be a wren with a large appetite now so that his mother will not be sad.

 She sits on the bedside chair. Eat up, she says. You must be starving. It's been a while since lunch.

Archie smiles, takes a pear slice, chews, forces himself to swallow. It's hard when he's not hungry. He must chew the pear to make it really mushy, so it slips down easily.

Read to me Mama, he says, wanting a distraction from the food.

She takes the book, opens it to the marker. Eat up, she says again, waiting for him to take a spoonful of carrot before she starts. Our favourite part, she says. The Piper at the Gates of Dawn. Then she reads.

Archie wants to stare out the window letting the words flow over and around him, the pictures taking shape. It's always a greenish shimmer he sees when she's reading: the lap of the river, air moving the grasses or leaves. He could be a slow moving dragonfly, a bubble forming on the river's skin, the little otter in Pan's arms. Just as he lifts the carrot to his mouth the bright orange goes into a slow fade to pale. He squints at it, blinks, takes a small mouthful, and it tastes the same. When he looks at it again it is just a normal carrot colour.

His mother's words are like hands stroking his face. The trees outside move gently in the breeze. He strains to see its colour but there is nothing but leaf and branch, one small bird taking flight. He watches until the bird disappears, and his eyes close. The words become a drone, then disappear.

Archie wakes to the light casting rods of gold onto the wall. It's a sunny day; he can feel its warmth and glow. When his mother comes in, she carries him to the toilet. He knows that Louis, Amir and Mason would be too heavy now to carry anywhere. Too embarrassed to let someone carry them to the toilet. His mother carries him back to bed, punches the cushions into shape, pulls the bedclothes over him. She opens the curtains. Look, she says, it's so lovely outside. Look at the red canna lilies in Mrs McKinnon's garden. Aren't they beautiful in the sun there. We should get some of those for right outside your window. Yes? Imagine that all those red heads nodding in the breeze, right there, she moves her hand to the expanse of the window, as if they are there already.

Archie nods.

Okay, breakfast. Some nice porridge, and some honey, hmm?

Archie nods again, tries out a smile. He feels odd this morning. Sleepy and floppy like a rag doll, although he slept well – dreamless, but a memory stains his recall, a memory of colour, of shapes floating, but no recall of what he has seen. His mother leaves to get his breakfast, the door closing on a momentary flash of pure brilliance. White, but like pearl. He stares blinking into its absence then turns away.

Out the window now the sun streams gold through the jacaranda across the road, carpet of purple beneath, covering the footpath. From his vantage point, the carpet looks soft and fluffy, as if it would be like landing in feathers if he fell from the tree, a flurry of purple rising around him on impact. Out there through the window is a morning that he feels no part of. It's as if Archie Griffiths does not exist for this golden morning. Only for here – this room, this bed. This head. So small, his world now. He feels it slip like night, or like a fish or water in his hands.

Seeing is all he has now. And the stories his mother reads to him, the ones he reads himself. He thinks of Harley, in the bed next to his in hospital, staring blindly at the ceiling. Blinded soon after birth, before he could even know the names or match them to the colours. Archie would try to describe the shapes of things, the colours, but Harley could only shake his head, I don't know, I don't know what you mean.

So you can't see any light at all?

Nothing. I can only see nothing.

What does it look like?

Harley thought a while. What does an ice-cream smell like? he asked.

Archie thought and thought. He tried words out in his head. But they weren't right. He understood then.

He looks out at the flowers along Mrs McKinnon's fence: the red and orange flare of colour, the fade, the build-up to brilliance again. Then the shimmer, the slow colour-fade, like dipping into bleach. He pictures his mother in the kitchen, standing at the stove, stirring his porridge. So long now since he's seen the kitchen, that small cramped space, chairs and a bench, the green cupboards with their shiny brown knobs. It would all be the same. Will all be there when he's no longer here, in his bed, with the window, the thinking darkness after he closes his eyes. He concentrates hard on the image of his mother, standing at the stove, spoon stirring around and around, her blue shirt tucked into her jeans, brown hair a mess of curls.

He's so tired now. Could sleep again though he's only just woken.

A hazy movement out the window, a sort of merge of everything he's looked on and over since the illness—no school, no friends visiting, only the doctor, his mother, the perfect square of the window. The haze moves in a column of air now, blue, then silver, then greenish gold. The red cannas his mother had so loved, are dots of fierce colour in this column of pale air. Then they melt. And the pearl shimmer moves like some crazy cyclone, round and around. There's a gap now, like the pure line of pearl and white between the door and door jamb. And light as air, he slips right through.

TOP ELEVEN

LANS FELBY

CLARE VALLEY, SOUTH AUSTRALIA

Crafting stories of all lengths, Lans Felby has a passion for writing diverse, complicated characters and exploring the world through their lens. When not penning new people into life, Lans spreads writing joy through coordinating an online writer's community. Xer writing nook is overrun with attention-seeking sighthounds.

JUST BLACK

People ask, is it just black. They ask, is it pure darkness, a sensation devoid of all colour and light and image? When they ask me, I can hear their sympathy—if I'm lucky, at least, it's sympathy. Sometimes it's pity. I don't really like it when it's pity.

Close your eyes, I tell them. It's my go-to reply. I can usually tell if they've done it before they tell me. I can feel it, the subtle shifts in the air between us as they either stare at me in shock and scorn or do as I suggest. People's attitudes can be read just as easily without needing to see their facial expressions. You just have to know what to listen for in their voices. Voices give away a lot.

When their eyes are closed, I ask, what can you see?

It's black. Almost everyone says simply, it's black.

Keep looking, I say. Just keep looking.

Some people lapse into contemplative silence, waiting for wonders to be revealed, some special knowledge they think I have simply because I cannot see. A lot of people don't do that. Instead, they'll ask on an incredulous breath, how am I supposed to look with my eyes closed?

Softly I reply again, just keep looking.

The thing about darkness is that often it's not just *black*. There are shadows in the darkness. There are waves of colour, dots and swirls that dance across the shifting shades of dark. Black is the complete lack of light. But being blind, at least for me, isn't the same as being cloaked in blackness. Maybe it's because I remember what light and colour and shape look like. Maybe it's because I used to see them, and my mind remembers what they are like. I don't know. Who of us can really speak about something outside of our personal experience? Not me, anyway. I'm not that enlightened. Not yet. Likely I never will be.

I wait for them to look into the shadows cast by their own eyelids, anticipating the moment of revelation. A lot of people have one—not all. I think it depends on how open they are to new experiences, how much imagination they have. Those who don't have it give up in a huff, frustrated words clipping my ears when they declare confidently, it's just black.

I shrug my left shoulder and tell them, then I can't explain what it's like for me being blind.

But it's not just black? they sometimes ask.

No, I say. It's not just black.

Then there's the others. My heart swells with delight when they gasp in soft surprise, a wondrous sound of realisation. Oh, they breathe. Oh, oh, oh, I see it. I see it now. It… dances. It's red and blue and bright, sparkling white. I can see it, they say.

Yes, I agree heartily. That's what I see. Light in the shadows. Brightness dimmed, but still inescapably there. A memory of colour, dynamic yet faded. It shines like rainbow obsidian, a shifting sheen of iridescence against the encompassing void of a true, perfect black.

They'll open their eyes then, and the next question is always the same. It's often phrased differently—Do you miss it? versus, Is it hard?—but the underlying meaning is always the same. It's a question I loathe absolutely. No matter how genuine their curiosity, how sincere their sympathy, it feels rude. Whatever words they use, that question is too personal.

Somehow it never feels like they're asking about me and my experience of losing my vision. What they're really doing is admitting their fear. Fear of losing the light. Fear of being shrouded in the darkness in a world designed to be seen.

You adapt, I tell them. You get used to it. You learn new ways of seeing.

Because the truth is, it's not the mystical shadows of the dregs of my sight that make me afraid. That's almost… cosmetic. No, the true fear is the darkness we hold inside ourselves. In material darkness, we can always find a way. We don't need to see, we can touch to find a path and uncover perils. We can listen for dangers. But the shadows that live inside us, those cannot be so easily escaped. They're much harder to outrun.

Going blind never scared me. Because I already knew a deeper darkness, a truer fear.

But of course, I don't tell them that.

Instead, I smile with a deliberate wistfulness and say, Yes, I miss it. Yes, it's hard. It's not a lie. But it's certainly not the whole truth.

TOP ELEVEN

GABI CADENHEAD
SYDNEY, NSW, AUSTRALIA

Gabi Cadenhead is a poet and composer living on unceded Gadigal and Wangal land. Their creative practice is one of intersections – between story and sound; between performance and protest; between embodiment, queerness and the sacred. Gabi's poetry has been published in #EnbyLife Journal, Insights Magazine *and* Sunder Journal, *and in 2022 they were selected for Express Media's* Toolkits: Poetry *program.*

SKY

the sky cracks open and I fall from it,
my first breath the dying whisper of a cloud.
lightning crackles from my bones;
they carry the power of me
which bursts forth, uncontainable.
I soften into rain, these tears
that hold my darkness and my strength.
watercolours tug the horizon into sunset,
pulsing with the gradient glow
at the heart of me.
I find myself there in the bleeding
of purple pink orange into pale green
and, with the universe, expand.

2
IMAGES

PHOTOGRAPH

MAYA LE HER

In the darkroom, our hands touch
And chemicals bleed together.
An image develops—

You stand in black
And white, arms lifted
As if to touch the ceiling.

Fingertips catching leaks
Of light from a cold source,
Where beauty broke through glass.

You become
Male, female, androgynous,
Shape-shifter. This is you,

Hand holding my hand to your face,
Your Adam's apple swollen
In beautiful rage. This is you,

Your head dipping back in sleep,
The hollow of your collarbone
Exposed to my gaze. This is you

On stage, body surging as if your form
Were made of water. Your mouth open
In a song without sound.

You blur at the edges, clarity forming
At your centre point. Yours is the definition
Of grace: beauty restrained.

Contained within the frame
Of our hands, chemicals balance
To form meaning from light and shadows.

DARK COUSIN

ROGER VICKERY

I snapped this shot with my Kodak Instamatic as you were surfacing from your dark room into the lemon light of a West Cork summer night.

I hadn't given notice, just shown up from across the Atlantic, right hand outstretched, camera cocked in my left like a dart, and pinned you with the Bay at your back.

Perhaps your day's catch of 24 x 24-inch visions from the Bay's Gulf Stream had already failed the test of your developing trays... *Truth tanks*, you called them... and been exposed as... *postcard pap?* Perhaps you'd been hitting the hard stuff you kept stashed behind your film canisters, been sucking on mints, so Morag wouldn't know?

A wet suit was stretched across your dive bag like a pet seal.

There was a slight shine in your eyes. A reflection from my Instamatic flash? Or the after-shock that you, the James Dean of photography in these parts, a taker—never the taken—was being mugged by a toy in the hands of a boy? It was hard to tell with you.

You were probably trying to pull me into focus, this lost cousin from the New World blathering away at you—who needs a pint or ten to net the slippery words of the land—about young ones long dead bearing our name who had been driven from the Bay when the Asiatic cholera was in their beds and the Famine's iron nails at their backs.

I've no time for barnacles, you said, and offered me a mint.

I had come to smell out Pedro's bones, his shining mystery bones.

He had floated in, the family story goes, on a galleon's spar and dug our clan's black eggs into the cove. But his tombstone sags above the Bay, hammered blank by Atlantic hooves. If we knew when and where he was born, we could follow that twine to his past.

Infra-red, you advised. Waiting until the bounce light was right, you shot the first man's stone with a roll of your smart bullets. Three days later our Rosetta stone was cracked.

B 1567 Cartagena.

We have you now, old Pedro, you muttered and looked away, as if embarrassed at this casual communion with spirits you chose in public to disdain.

I wish I could as easily, dark cousin, poured developer across the negatives beneath your surface.

I was blathering on about some near-death escape on the hippie trail in Sarawak, Laos or the Yucatan and you looked at me as if I had a hoard of Celtic silver at my feet.

Your worst dives are when you swim through visions the Gulf Stream bestows: Albino parrot fish, shoals of red blenny, basking sharks, whiting, hake, coral that could have been dusted with rainbow icing, anemones rightly named jewel, dahlia or plumose... and all you have to scoop this glory is a wobbling lump of water-proofed Minolta.

Later, looking into the truth tanks at your pathetic catch, you always needed a drink.

Seamus, a brogue clown from central casting, showed up at the local and began reeling in your twine, framing you as a Playboy of the West Cork World, giving as for instance the time the two of you were thrashing a stolen boat towards Dingle.

Navigation lights doused, pissed as pipers, bound for a beach party hosted by a coven of naked women...

Until you gripped his shoulder and led him wincing to the door, saying:

We are strangers now, with a nasty shake in your throat.

It was a bad Irish joke, the nature of your death. Skewered like a seal with your own spear gun.

Accident or design?

It was hard to tell with you.

On the day of the wake, Seamus slipped through Morag's picket and began sharing blue anecdotes of you. I was hungry for some focus on the roaring boy who yearned to be away from the Bay that held him in irons, lost and deep as the wrecks that lie beneath it.

But I came away empty.

The new family plot, anchored in the flat heart of the town, safe from the hooves of Atlantic gales, is far below. Hoping for a bit of blather, I have puffed up to the headland to squat beside old Pedro's re-cut marker stone.

The Guinness cream clouds overhead put me in mind of a school of albino parrot fish gliding from a net.

Or am I overlaying a 24 x 24-inch vision of the Bay, that only you could catch?

The truth is, dark cousin, you stayed because your prints were never clearer than here, swimming in this lemon light.

FADE OUT: THE FORT NEPEAN TUNNELS

SUZI MEZEI

Before our descent, a woman steps from the bus
into December glare, opens a gold parasol, adjusts shades.
On matted coastal floor, sightseers weave like hexapods
in hats 'round information plaques and cement-gagged
cannons. In pairs and small cliques visitors wilt

like maladapted blooms at rough-hewn picnic tables,
under attack from blowflies. Deep in tunnels, there's
a muffled crush of errant sand underfoot, our voices distort,
collide on curved steel walls and disappear inside the dim.
Every word down here grows wings, becomes a blue wren

or a whistler, thrashes between inverts and arcs before
it's lost amongst vacant chambers where artillery once
slept shallow; an eye always open. A soldier's ghost shoves past,
we brush shoulders, I follow him up atrophied cement steps
through musty haze, share for a moment the darkness

of a soldier's days. I can scarcely imagine what happened next.
Here, light pours through an emplacement; here, he positions
his rifle. Outside, white correa and sticky daisy tangle amongst
tea-tree, tiger snakes leave behind their rotted husks, tourists
meander, water-bottles in hand and beyond that, The Heads

drag blue water out to distant lands. Time to go; perhaps
I echo what the soldier once spoke. I leave him to defend
what I did not; I cannot fathom what he lost. And when I emerge,
I stretch, wrapped in radiant sun, the burrows of war an
unseen backdrop in auto-focussed snaps of the Fort.

BUSHFIRES

SUZANNA FITZPATRICK

I watch the blaze online, a screensaver
of pixel embers. You pack bags,
spread water where you can, the flames

just miles away. Humidity
and temperature, the vagaries of wind:
these are the measurements of likely loss.

Here, rain and sudden thaw breed floods
whose footage laps your fires repeatedly
but can't extinguish them. It makes no sense.

I light a candle, hesitate –
stare at the match as it translates to black,
then blow it out. I wish the same for you.

THE SUNDAY AFTER

LIAM BOYLE

1.

We're on the footpath outside the Genoa café,
febrile this day of mourning and anger.
The British Embassy was burned last night.

We're all friends here, the gang.
We've shared cokes and jokes and cigarettes.
We've danced and laughed together.

Carmel backs Jane up against the wall:
"Your fault, you English bastard. Thirteen dead!"
Jane, stunned, hands up, palms out, "Not me."

We get between them, calm the moment,
then turn away in silent confusion,
not sure what just happened.

2.

Next Sunday, a helicopter overhead
repeats its message over the roar of its rotors,
"this march is illegal, disperse, go home."

I have hitched to the border, walked to the town.
My thermos gives pause at an army checkpoint. I pass.
In the town centre I see a platform and loudspeakers.

I follow others to find the assembly point, a milling crowd
soon pressed into serried rows by earnest marshals.
We set off in silence.

3.

The army has blocked the road; we're still moving forward.
Directions are shouted back, "turn left at the barricade."
We turn into a narrow lane, break ranks in the jostle.

We're elated, confrontation averted, we've shown them.
I hear a Kerry voice, "I'm ready if they try anything," he chuckles,
gesturing at a gun in his jacket pocket. I shake my head. Incensed.

We come to a field. The real meeting place; town was a decoy.
"Move on; make room for those behind you."
Speeches: Mumble mumble, we are strong. We shall overcome.

4.

Local women move through the crowd, on a mission.
Are you from the South? You hitched all this way?
Have you eaten? Would you like some tea?

I'm led to a nearby house, seated in the back kitchen,
with a window view of the meeting field.
Speeches are ending; the crowd is dispersing.

They feed the boy from the South, as much as he can manage.
"Thank you for being here," they say.
Afterwards, I hitch home – in the dark.

3
PLEASURE
& PAIN

MEDICINAL

ANGELA COSTI

A response to Mary Oliver's poetry, in particular 'The Summer Day'

on a day her bones and organs spasmed
in the way they needed
with what he'd done to her
as a child
she wrote
one word into a phrase into a stanza into a poem
it got published   read   shared   recited
became a mantra
then a belief
for thousands sitting in circles
opening their chests
to finally breathe out the forbidden

                in my twenties
                we got married
                and proceeded to grow fond of each other
                year after year
                I released the moaning and bickering
                by taking slow walks among tree multitudes
                so many walks hoping green would calm
                the simmering arguments
her poem grew into a belief
for a girl to carry as they study physics
for a boy to study as they write in their diary
                I too joined a circle
                unbuttoned my shirt
                showed strangers my scars
                they greeted them like old friends
                as I told my story of a child
                with father
                who couldn't restrain a slap

a mantra for
a woman to travel with the lightest of baggage to locate her ancestral tombs
a man to fall in love with the duster and take it travelling from shelf to sill

> still illness refused divorce
> my tumours disguised the child injuries
> bloodied mouth   bruised bottom
> the shock congeals into the unsaid

a faith
as a woman riddled with dementia remembers her birthday and
her ninety year old husband bakes an opera cake to celebrate

> when I walk
> in waving grass
> there is no stewing grunt
> churning my stomach
> I share her poem
> among the ferns   leaves   bark   sap
> hear honey eaters sing   louder
> find myself dappled   in light

for the shadow becomes shade

IN THE BAR MY MUM USED TO WORK

TIM LOVEDAY

the smoke never shows on a ceiling that colour. decades cling to
lungs like smouldering to glass. & still, i hear the men talking as
if they can rewrite the prize horse with a pint, the mean bet that
turned their futures to shadows, to ash.

there in the alcove i once called my childhood, an eternity of
light wept into the soggy coaster or clear as a looking glass on
the varnish, my eyes squint through the ventilator's hazy as
someone wins the feature & an old woman cries, not once but
many times.

my mother knew the right beer before a note hit the bar. the
twitch of an eyebrow, a threat not a courteously. certain names,
she was told, kept the coppers at bay, so she learnt to say *locals*.
she, in turn, was a mother of sorts. give 'em pride. give 'em
place. listen. that's all they wanted like anyone else. her father
was a drunk, so perhaps she saw the trick for what it was. no one
called this bleating. no one called this place pews.

me, no bigger than a hangnail, 12 ounces that head-butted the
rim, i watched with astonishment, as these men emptied
themselves with the emptying of a glass. i wish i could say i
didn't admire them—but two decades later, i'm still searching
for the men who talk as if all men are granted.

THE CHRISTMAS PARTY

OWEN DWYER

Carrying a curry and a kebab in a white plastic sack, I made my way through groups of drunks, some singing, some otherwise, until I eventually found the red brick in Streatham and shoved the gate to the garden flat with my hip. The kebab was for Joe—he'd insisted I buy it as we left the pub. This despite him going back to Rosie's flat. Some English Rosie, who lived at the end of the yellow brick road that stretched from Dublin to London. A Rosie who had sex in her flat whenever she felt like it. The curry was for me, the *ruby murray*, bought because the rhyming slang made it delicious, though I'd never tasted Indian food.

It was Christmas week, and I was on a break from the tedium of Dublin and my father's disapproval; if I liked what I saw I was going to stay and look for work. Everything was new that week and I was high on alcohol-fuelled exuberance, as I heaved open the door of the squat. A crack of light from the street put her into relief against the gloom, causing her to look up at me and nothing concurrently. My eyes adjusting, I made out a black T-shirt draped on wasted shoulders, out of which her neck grew like a pale root to support her shadowy head. Thin white arms, scarred and listless, lay like crossbones on her lap. She had been sitting alone in the dark, on a battered beanbag, surrounded by shards of charred tinfoil. Mutilated tinsel.

'I'm Eoin, Joe's friend,' I said. 'Season's greetings.'

'I know who the fuck you are,' she said. 'You're another drunken paddy. Full of bitter and takeaway slop.'

'And you're the junky,' I said, finding the wall with my back and sliding down to her level. 'Joe warned me about you.'

'I'd prefer to be a junkie than an ignorant paddy beer-guzzler,' she said, which might have been a joke if it wasn't for her voice and expression. Contempt— it was my first real experience of it.

'Look love.' I said, exasperated. 'There's a difference. Getting drunk and eating takeaways is one thing, locking yourself up all day and injecting heroin into your veins is a different story.'

'Is it?' She seemed pleased by my outburst. 'What's the difference?'

'One kills you. The other just gives you a headache and diarrhoea.'

'Oh please. Any idiot knows ten times more people die as a result of alcohol poisoning than heroin abuse. Not to mention the wife beating, car accidents, hooliganism and violence outside clubs and bars. Over eighty per cent of violent crime is attributed to alcohol abuse. You're just off the fucking boat, what would you know? They don't tell you anything in Ireland.'

'That's a load of crap.'

'Why?'

'Just look at you and your boyfriend. You never go anywhere—you never *do* anything… where is Romeo anyway?' She lifted her eyes to the ceiling to indicate the room upstairs, where I'd seen him comatose on a mattress earlier.

'Napping.'

'I thought he'd be out providing entertainment for the elderly living alone, this Christmas.'

'Oh, you're funny too. We don't go out because there's nowhere to go and nothing to do when you get there.'

I snapped the ring on a can of cider, opening it at my fourth attempt, then lit a cigarette.

'You could do a day's work, pay your own way.'

'Nobody works here. You and your friends, the Irish drunks, you come over here collecting the dole in different places, screwing the government.'

'Jesus, it's only the English government. It's not like we owe Thatcher anything. And anyway, I do work—at home.' She leaned over, took the cigarette from my fingers without asking, before settling into her bean bag and pluming smoke at the dark ceiling.

'You're pretty stupid, do you know that?' Drunk as I was, I knew she was too clever for me and that any argument I gave would be twisted and thrown back in my face. She was looking for trouble in her bored midnight, with her boyfriend on a mattress upstairs and me, the red faced virgin fresh off the boat. 'Yes,' she repeated. 'You're stupid as fuck. If you think there is any point to work. What did your parents ever get from work? A lifetime of slaving to pay the mortgage on a semi-detached? Ulcers from worrying where the car repayments are coming from? Scrimping and saving and the only thing they enjoy is getting drunk and making a fool of themselves doing the hokey-pokey at the office Christmas party?'

'That's what it's all about.'

'Another joke. You're on a roll.'

'You're saying heroin is an alternative to that,' I said, becoming serious. 'A whole other life?'

'Does it matter what I'm saying? You wouldn't understand anyway. Your mind's closed.' She scowled and sucked—reviewed me through mean little eyes.

'Well then. Why don't you tell me what it's like?'

'What?'

'Heroin.'

'Jesus. Listen to him.'

Smoking in the silence, she became detached in the way I was beginning to understand only junkies could. It didn't matter what time of year it was or even what planet we were on.

The partying clumps staggering down Streatham High Street roaring 'Happy Christmas' might have been giant ants with their heads on fire, for all she knew or cared. She was in a universe of her own, surrounded by whatever demons put her there. Still clinging to my own reality, I looked around the dark cavern of the squat and wondered if there was anywhere less Christmassy I could have put myself. My father would be sitting in front of the TV at home, dinner on his lap, wishing my mother was alive. I might have made more of an effort and decided I would do so in the future. In the meantime, me and the junkie were in opposite corners. There was no sign of life in the space between us. I wondered about the boyfriend. There wasn't a sound from upstairs either—he might have been dead.

'Death. That's what it's all about,' she said. 'Death.'

'What?' My turn now to show contempt, which I did with a shake of the head and an affected snort. By this, she seemed amused and reciprocated with a sneer of her own, trumping my attempt. She was in no hurry to break the silence, which re-established itself and which she seemed to control. I drank, lit another smoke and tried to look like I would be bored by anything she might say, while really wondering if the curry had gone cold.

'You know every time you inject, it could be your last,' she said, quietly. 'But you don't care. It's like all your Christmases have come together, the pleasure. It's like the best orgasm you've ever had, if you've ever really had one, multiplied by ten, by a hundred, all over your body. It completely consumes you. Nothing else matters or ever did, but the pleasure. And the only thing you know, is that you've never experienced pleasure like this before and never will again, without a fix. I get more pleasure from one hit than you'll get in a lifetime. That's why we do it. We're not trying to change the world; we just want to be left alone. It doesn't matter where we are or what happens to us, or anyone else. Nothing matters.

And it's when you reach that nothing matters part you realise what a waste all the rest is. How futile the world is; how ridiculous people like you are. Your prejudices, your narrowminded ignorance, your complete incomprehension of everything. Your whole life will be one long drawn-out drudge. Oh, you'll convince yourself that there are high points. Meeting some inane bitch you see as your soul mate; the birth of a sprog. But they'll all let you down in time, and you'll let them down. You'll die years from now at the end of a long, uneventful life. Mine will be half as long but with twice the enjoyment. I'll have exhausted the pleasure gland and refused to engage with the drudgery. I'll never compromise— I'll never let myself be sucked in by the system, by dullards like you. It's all to do with time, you want it—I don't.'

'So that's what it's all about is it? Pleasure. And here was me thinking there was some great philosophical reason. But it's as simple as that. You're a glutton.'

'I'm not the only one, am I? You come over here, you and your like, not because you want a career or even to work, but because you want all those gratifications denied you on that backward island you come from. You're guests of the nation abusing its hospitality because of your greed—for money, for sex, for cheap beer and cigarettes. Even take-away curry is a big deal to troglodytes. And all so that you can go back after Christmas acting the big man, with all that sex experience and money to burn holes in your pockets. It's about egosatiation, being able to say to your mates that you got laid or that you had an argument with some junkie bitch in a squat and ripped her to shreds. You're trying to denigrate and dismiss me for no other reason than to satiate your fragile ego. But it doesn't matter. Someone like you could never matter to me; could never impact me in any way. I am free from inhibition and disappointment because you-just-don't-matter.' I was getting upset now. Not just because of what she was saying but because of the way she was saying it. It was as if I was a worthless piece of shit to her, and to think that anybody could have that low an opinion of me, especially when we'd just met, disturbed me. But I kept talking, not wanting her to see how wounded I was.

'What about your man upstairs? If nothing matters, what are you doing with him?' She reached her cigarette hand out and nodded at a can of cider, which I opened and handed to her.

'You wouldn't understand.'

'You can't keep dismissing my questions by telling me I'm too stupid to understand the answer.' She laughed.

'We're in this together, Jim and me. This was his thing and now it's our thing. It's what we do. There's nothing else to it, nothing else to know. Why do you want to know anyway? Why should you care?'

'You're right. I don't care.' I'd finally had enough. 'I'm going to bed.'

'Already? I was half thinking of screwing you.'

I did not find her attractive, she was gaunt, dirty and smelled, but I was twenty and drunk. She bit and scratched as we made love—made small, annoyed noises in the back of her throat—resenting me for not giving her enough pleasure, for not being heroin. Afterwards she retreated to the corner with the beanbag and watched as I ate the curry with a plastic spoon I found in the bag. While some drunk outside sang I'm Dreaming of a White Christmas off key and in a lamenting voice.

Years later, I met Joe for a drink in Dublin. It was the late nineties and he had just returned with the receding emigration wave to what was the beginning of an economic boom. We spoke about our respective careers, kids, old friends and about my father who had passed away the previous year. We eventually got on to London and to the week I spent with him in the squat. I asked about the girl.
'Carolyn? The once and famous junkie?' he said, remembering her more easily than I thought he would. 'She got her act together big time after the sprog. Gave up the drugs, left your man Jim behind in the squat. Then he died, poor bastard. I had to call the ambulance, and we all had to get out. We were interrogated by the police, had to give blood samples and everything.'
    'Jesus. But tell me, what happened to this Carolyn?'
    'We kept in touch for a while. She ended up getting a job in social services in Brixton, working with disadvantaged kids or something. Used her degree, went on to do a Masters, in Social Science, something like that. The last I heard from her was a letter inviting me to her wedding, which I couldn't make for some reason. Said she'd met her soul mate and that I'd really like him—the usual. The funny thing about her was that she was always full of brains. Full of crap but full of brains. The kid really sorted her out, although how Junky Jim managed to knock her up is a mystery.'
    'Are you sure it was him knocked her up?'
    'Sure, who else could it have been? They didn't leave the squat for months. And who else would have touched her back then anyway?'
    'Who indeed?' I said—Gobbling down my pint as the expression on his face changed.

OUTFOXING MERRI CREEK

VERONICA TROUP

half away
    from tourists
and 24 hour service

      right leg over leg
    threads the cross bar
        chasing rain

past the town hall clock
    neon burgers and
bone stutter trams

            air low-slung
         around me
          of earth and fuel
         and eddied leaves

     through the park

late walkers knock about
    dogs skip frisbee shadows

         in this ink-blot darkness
       of baby baths and bedtimes
       lights flick off with a sigh and
       cling to adult conversation

hugs me darker still
    the always fear
    under the sling-shot station pass
    I pedal faster

           just make it to the main road

at the bridge
    bat wings confuse
    against the night sky

        I swerve the local
    people full
    trivia laugher falters
        out the smokers' door

across the street
        to my flat
    the lights are off
       and I remember

                there is no need to hurry

UP ON THE MOORS

SOPHIE O'HAGAN

I'm up nearly as high as the clouds, cheeks red and battered from the wind, my skin tight to my face. Each step forward along this muddy track takes me higher. It's not raining but I'm soaked. Under my layers it's from sweat and outside those three coats I have on (one for warmth, one for the wind, one for the rain) it's from the foggy clouds of moisture. They drench me as I forge a path through, socks soaked despite my boots. Hands red despite my gloves. A November moorland with typical weather. There's barely any colour but odd glimpses of purply green stand out from the brown and grey of everything else.

My trousers cling to me as I plough on soaping up with each movement. You might think that I am in misery hiking in this weather but to me this is what life's about. It's on hikes like this that I feel truly alive. I can walk through my problems as everything else falls away and if it's too heavy to carry up this hill. It's not coming; I'll see it on the way down.

Lights flash. Noise, an overpowering amount of noise shakes me as I'm jostled about by crowds pushing and shoving. The rain drizzles down forming puddles in the gaps between cobbles in the streets. People groan as water splashes up at them when they walk. Everyone is seeking shelter under bags or flimsy jackets.

'Why am I here again?' I say turning to the woman next to me in a black mini skirt with a strangely cropped and simultaneously oversized red corduroy shirt.

'Because I never see you anymore!' she replies with a slightly whining tone. I look around me at huddles of people queuing to get into this club and wonder if she's realised why yet.

'Maybe it's because this isn't really my scene anymore.'

'It'll be fun. Just enjoy it.' I don't need to respond to this because as she closes her mouth the lad in front of us conveniently vomits all over the floor and wall… and himself… narrowly missing her boots. It has the effect of illustrating my point perfectly. I simply raise my eyebrows at her with a slight wrinkle of my nose as the smell starts to permeate the air. She merely hops over the vomit and passes the group of lads being, shall we say, escorted (that's probably the nicest way of saying it) out of sight.

'That doesn't usually happen,' she says, acting all coy and innocent. Loosely translated, that means it always happens, which is no great secret.

The rain gets heavier as we get to the entrance. I really should've brought a coat but that isn't what the 'cool kids' do.

I come out of the clouds and into the muted sunlight. A touch brighter than it had been only a few moments before but only because the sky is now a lighter shade of grey. There's one less cloud between me and the sun. I catch my breath for a second; there's only a short way to go before the cairn on top. I think I'll properly stop there. I keep on going up the hill, the path shifting and squelching beneath my feet. Sometimes walking backwards helps me get up a steep bit but after taking one step back and almost landing, splat bang, on my rear end I decide not to tempt fate with that. I'd rather just be drenched than drenched and coated in mud.

It's getting windier as I get nearer the top, which isn't really surprising. My hair is tied tightly into a plaited bun and tucked into a green and blue Nordic knitted hat; my only worry is that I'll lose it. I don't want to have to go chasing after it, but my mum made it for me, so I would probably have to.

The few trees around are bare of leaves and look black against the sky, leaning down over the edge, blown this way and that by the wind.

We head over to the bar leaning against the side and trying to catch someone's eye. After five or probably closer to ten minutes we get served and are handed a glass each (paying an exorbitant amount for it, in addition to paying almost the same amount to even get in). Kate (my friend) drags us to the middle of the dance floor. There's about enough room to put your arm directly up, or if you're feeling crazy, jump up and down—just make sure you don't land on anyone's toes. That sounds easy enough, but what do I do with my drink while this is going on? Kate doesn't have that issue after downing her double something and lemonade, I, however, don't want to do that, so it takes me a bit longer to finish mine, and when I have, I'm still stuck with the cup.

Having reached the cairn, I plop myself down on a tree root and look at the view. A spectacular greyscale of clouds. Utterly breathtaking, but then again, that could just be the wind; so much for the Great British countryside. I reach for my water bottle to take a big swig, but remembering the lack of toilets in the car park, I only take a sip. I undo the clasp on my dry bag backpack thing and shelter the opening from the weather, grabbing my lunch out, to avoid flooding the bag. From out of my lunch bag comes half a tuna sandwich, a chocolate bar, and a satsuma. I'd gotten a bit peckish in the car on the way, so there is only half the sandwich left.

A feast for a king, or at least enough food to get me home without my stomach complaining. I eat it quickly, then set off again, checking which way to go on the map; after all, it'd be boring to go back the way I came. The sun is starting to come out, teasing me from just behind the clouds, like a parent entertaining their baby with a game of peekaboo.

The most exposed bit is along the top, so as I drop down walking at a decent pace, I start to warm up quite quickly. It hasn't started raining again, so off comes a layer here and a little further along a layer there. All I can see surrounding me for miles is purple heather only just ankle height and wobbling, like jelly, in the wind.

I understand the need for smoking areas but why did the geniuses at this club decide it had to be inside? I'm trapped in a room full of people, squished in like sardines, more smoke than breathable air. Thanks to vapes there's a whole array of smells: you've got your typical nicotine, then there's candy floss, blue raspberry, tutti frutti, marshmallow (all the sickly sweet ones), and every now and then there's a faint smell of cannabis—conveniently no one's quite sure where that one's coming from.

'You got a smoke' some guy says, the words tripping as they fall out of his mouth.

'Nah. My mate might do though.'

'It's okay, love. I'll find someone else.' He staggers off through the crowd, bumping off people as though he's in a pinball machine. I'm genuinely amazed as I watch him walk away; chances are with all that swaying, he's walked twice the distance. I shake my head half bemused and half confused and turn back round to Kate.

Who seems to have wandered off. Great!

All it took was turning one bend, and suddenly, the green fields of the Yorkshire Moors have laid themselves like a blanket at my feet. The path twists as it slopes away back down into the valley, somehow bypassing the rain and clouds I'd come up through earlier. They must've just blown away. I plod downhill, placing one foot carefully in front of the other, with my knees taking most of the strain. I've always preferred going up to coming down. It might be because, going up, I have the rest of the hike ahead, whereas coming down, I'm only headed home back to everything I was hiking away from. It seems to me the same as people running away from their problems, but they'll always catch up with you in the end.

As I reach the bottom of this particular hill, I see a little brook chattering and giggling through the smallest of valleys. A few stones, that are half underwater because of the rain, seem to be the only way across. I tap the first one with my toe, half tempted just to plunge on through (I am already soaked)—it seems stable enough. I do the same thing with the second and third and then the fourth. The fifth one's a tad wobbly but close enough to the bank that it isn't a problem. Having reached the other side, I look up. I didn't realise when planning this route that I had an additional hill to go up, much less one that climbed 300 meters in 200 meters of distance (give or take). To be fair that may have been why I hadn't noticed it on the map. Oops. Up I go, zigzagging this near cliff face that I have led myself to. It takes a lot of energy that I hadn't stored up for, but it isn't exactly like I have a choice at this point.

At the top I can see where all those clouds had gone. They wait for me, grey and ominous, having sunken to the bottom of the valley.

I look around for her, text her, ask the staff if they've seen her but to no avail. She's not in the toilets, the smoking area, or at any of the bars. I call her frantically to check she's okay. As much as I don't want to be here, and her disappearing gives me the opportunity to leave; I really do need to find her first.

I stand next to a bouncer outside calling her, eventually, she picks up.

Apparently, she's run into a guy she hooks up with and has left with him. I hang up on her and leave. I can feel my blood boiling as I navigate the midnight streets, taking my regular cut-throughs, despite the hour. I just want to get home, wash this night off me and get some sleep. After all, I need to be getting up early tomorrow, to head out on my hike.

It takes me longer than it should have to realise I'm not alone. It takes me longer still to realise that whoever it is who's behind me is following me. I've been looking at the pavement since I left the club and it's just dawning on me as I leave the brightly lit streets of the inner city that I shouldn't be walking home alone.

At the top of this new hill, there's a different wind, more powerful and less erratic. It's blowing me back the way I came rather than towards the car park, which is almost in sight. My feet and legs are starting to tire a bit, and I slow down to give them a little break. I don't like slowing down. It means I think more. I don't want to think. Not today.

My phone's in my bag, and so are my keys so I can grab them and that might get him to leave me alone. However, if they're in my hands would I be able to push him off? If I slow down to get them out, will he take that as an opportunity? Do I run? No. He's faster. Do I shout? Well, he's not done anything. Not yet. Maybe he just lives near me, and he'll set off in a different direction soon. I'm sure I'll be fine. I'll just keep walking quickly and watch for any shadows creeping up on me. Just keep going, you're almost home.

I speed up again and face the wind directly. I think the path should turn in a minute and head around a bend. That might give me a bit of protection from this gale. Fingers crossed. I really should start checking the weather forecast before going on hikes. It would be a sensible thing to do.

I've been out for five hours, with less than one left to go. Not too bad then. I can have a hot drink and go to the loo when I'm done. There's nothing wrong with going home. Is there? I find a boulder to hide behind and throw my layers back on to try and keep me toasty. I may be less aerodynamic as a puffy ball of coats but at least I'm stylish. A wry smile briefly touches my lips before disappearing again. My eyes water as I push forward (I'm sure it's just from the wind).

I keep to streets, no more alleyways and cut throughs tonight. Main roads only. He's still getting closer but hasn't made a move yet. Maybe I'm just being paranoid.

There's a little alley to the back of the row of terraces I live on. The bins are kept there, tucked neatly behind out of view of the street.

He's practically breathing down my neck at this point, so close I swear I can feel his sweat dripping onto my back. I can smell his cologne. I hear him panting to keep up with me. Just keep walking, I tell myself. You're almost there. There's no doubt in my mind but I'm too close to run. I left it too late. I'm sure.

As I get to that alley, with all the bins, his arm clamps around me. At the same time, his other hand goes over my mouth. I try to kick him as he lifts me off the floor and to the back of the row of houses. I try to scream. I try to push him off. I give up. His shadow merging with mine. My eyes tearing up. My body limp and lifeless. I'm being spat on by the rain.

He leaves.

It starts raining again as the car park comes into sight. I do a bit of a half-run and a bit of a half-walk so I don't actually get anywhere faster, and I look a tad weird, but it makes me feel as though I will. The sun is now well and truly behind the smears of charcoal that are painted across the sky. I get back to the car still drenched from the first part of the walk, and more so with that final shower. I dry myself off and change. Then sit behind the wheel and stare unblinking at the top of the moor. The only place where it's not raining.

THE GUY WITH THE WOUND

KAREN LEA ARMSTRONG

He is quiet
Calls me ma'am
barely flinches
as I unwind gauze,
swab, inject
He faces the screen,
The pastor promoting eternal life

Who stabbed you, I ask,
(As if a neck slash,
near-miss of every life-preserving vessel
is common as the sky)

A shrug beneath the sterile field:
I'd have won
if he didn't have the knife.

Stitching now,
above the knob of curved collarbone
below the sparsely stubbled chin;
He rubs his forehead,
right-hand knuckles
crusted, oozing.

Acknowledgement is silent:
a suture
(or twelve)
can't really heal this wound,
that tracks through viscera and space,
feral preservation.

The day has closed its eyes.
Can you see? He asks,
pulls the cord on the wall
so we share
a smudged imperfect light

CUT FROM THE SAME CLOTH

PAT ABRAHAM

'Welcome to the sticks.'

When Lara peered up at the doctor, what she noticed first was his forced, almost shy grin. He shook her hand a little too clumsily. Much younger than she had expected—perhaps just five years older than her. She followed him to a shiny red car he'd parked outside the small country town airport and froze when he asked her to take the wheel.

'There's nothing like it in fifty kilometers of this dump town,' he said, rubbing the bonnet. Noticing her hesitation, he added, a little gently: 'You've got years before you can dream of owning a car like this. You aren't here just to learn to stitch wounds. Live a little, Lara.' The keys jingled as they flew through the air. She caught them with a clink.

She sat in the sleek leather seat and placed her hands on the steering wheel. Soon she was moving along the unsealed road, travelling at what her old man used to call 'granny speed.' She was okay with driving slow—what could be worse than crashing your supervisor's car, on the first day of your posting?

The doctor liked talking or at least having someone to talk to. He introduced himself as Finley. 'The first thing you need to understand,' he said, 'is I don't care much for medicine; I'm working so I can stop working, if you catch my drift. I've got things going on the side.' She nodded and tried to look sympathetic. He told her to drive faster. 'This town is basically a dump,' he continued,' but there are a couple of places around worth visiting, I could show you if you want.' She kept her eyes on the road, her mouth glued shut. It would be a long eight weeks.

'Faster,' he said, leaning forward and tapping the glove box like a drum. 'If you can't let your hair down here, you can't anywhere. Not a kangaroo in sight. Live a little, Lara.'

She felt a telescoping pull in her gut as the car accelerated. She could hardly believe it was her own foot pushing the pedal. A wild thrill washed over her, like the downward arc of a roller coaster ride. By the time she registered the thud and blur of a small brown body hitting the bumper, smacking against the windscreen, and bouncing lifelessly onto the roadside, whatever it was had become a full stop in the rearview mirror.

She kept driving, and it was a long time before Finley spoke. 'Probably a roo,' he said quietly. 'Forget about it. Keep going.'

They passed acacias and eucalypts on the winding country road girded by crimson dirt. The trees were there before, but now it was the long shadows they formed on the road that Lara noticed most. Student and doctor drove in silence, granny speed. Breathing had become hard—the cool air suddenly felt like thick goo that would only reach her lungs through force of effort. What had she done back there?

A numb tide washed over her and separated her from the world outside the car. She shook her head and tried to repossess herself. But this was a new kind of fear, and she had no bearings by which to crawl out. What had she done back there?

'The people in this town,' Finley said. 'How do I put this delicately? They don't always have the same notion of life that you and I might have. They are good people, don't get me wrong. But...'

Lara heard sounds coming out of Finley's mouth, but they were just a cold hum, hardly words. She had a vague sense she ought to be disgusted by what he was implying—but had she not just done a far worse thing? But what thing? How much worse?

'What I'm saying,' Finley continued, 'is whatever it was back there that you hit—don't lose sleep over it. No one else will. And you still have a degree you need to. . .'

She braked and spun the wheel, hanging a sharp U-turn. Rubber on road pierced through the silent night, and the black silhouettes of the acacias and eucalypts reared into focus. It was dark and the shadows were gone. Finley pounded the dashboard with a closed fist, screaming at her to turn back around. 'It was only a roo.' he shouted, 'Don't be stupid. Only a roo...'

Lara drove on until they reached the body.

Crouching down and peering at the corpse, prodding it with a crooked stick, Finley looked up at Lara. 'Dead as an autopsy,' he said, 'Probably stray. Nothing to do but bury it.'

Her hands were shaking. She had been taught to deal with far worse than this. Diagnosing death and triaging the maimed in loud, stinking, chaotic conditions. But this was different. She did this.

'Couldn't it be someone's pet?' she said, voice strained. 'We have to tell them.'

Finley scowled. 'Not many pets in this town,' he said. 'Chances are it's a stray. We ought to bury it though. If we don't, I can tell you're going to have an opinion about it. This whole month, I'm going to see that sour face of yours, those big sad eyes.'

Sighing, he rolled up the sleeves of his work shirt and took a large white hospital towel from the boot of his car. He knelt on the dirt with one knee and wrapped the dog in it. He did it slow, respectful, the way a midwife swaddles a newborn. Something about the tender way he handled the body was what made Lara cry—silently, the way she cried while watching a sad film in a cinema, without anybody noticing.

The closest house was half a football field away from the road. They trudged towards it through dry grass that went halfway up to their knees. As the house came into view, a boxy weatherboard on stilts, Finley revealed that the man who lived there was his patient.

'Crazy fella', he said. 'Mental health up to the eyeballs. Stockman or some such, fancies himself an artist on the side. Tried to neck himself last winter. This'll be a lesson for you, Lara, a real treat for your bleeding heart.'

The paint on the outside walls was peeling badly, but what seized Lara was a tall stack of egg cartons piled up on the front porch. There was no light coming from the house and the silhouette of the cartons looked grotesque, like a crooked tower from a fairy tale. There was no doorbell but soon after Finley knocked, a thin man about forty with stubble and thinning hair and crooked teeth appeared. His dull eyes lit up when he saw the doctor.

'Light of my eyes, he saved my life,' the stockman said, beaming. 'Without his magical hands, I'd be under by now.' He pulled up the sleeve of his flannel shirt and showed Lara the proof, a keloid scar which he explained was a cancer the doctor had cut out.

The stockman then noticed the towel Finley was carrying, and reached out for it, but Finley held it back and shook his head.

'Maggs, look, I bring sad news. I'm afraid I hit a stray dog outside,' he said, waving in the direction of the road. He peeled back a corner of the towel, revealing a whisper of the dog's face. 'It was dark, and I didn't see it. We've got to bury it now.'

Lara, numb, searched Finley for a clue to this turn, but all she found was that hardnosed face, which now said: play along, don't go rogue on me again.

'Maggs, is it—is it your dog?' Lara asked.

'No, miss,' the stockman said, his voice flatter now. He was still looking at the dog though, and his voice was a lot softer than before. 'I mean, I may've seen her here and there, over the years. Not a pet though, miss. Landlord don't allow pets here.'

He receded into the house, and when he returned, he brought two rusty shovels. He kept one for himself and gave the other to the doctor, who immediately passed it to Lara. 'You make your bed, you lie in it,' Finley said. 'That's what my old man always told me.'

'Mine too,' Lara said, wrapping her hands around the cool wood and squeezing tight. She realised she had never buried anything in her life, except toys in the sand as a child. Still, she was glad to have something solid for her restless hands to hold. A meaningful job to do.

They walked in tandem through an off-kilter side gate to the backyard of the property. Lara and Maggs set to digging in the far corner, next to a sloping grey fence and large woodland tree framing the half moon. Lara had most of her life regarded 'moonlight' as some sort of trick word, a folk belief of those who did not study science; but here she could do nothing but regard the moon, even the half that was showing, with awe for what it allowed her to see. The yard looked down upon an endless slope of pastures.

Cicadas riffed and the wind sang as they dug. Finley gazed at the sky and whistled an old hymn that Lara recognised from her boarding school days. She realised, with something bordering on disgust, that she and Finley had probably been raised in similar circumstances, back in the city. To Maggs, the two of them must appear cut from the same cloth.

The dirt was hard and did not want to give way. The pungent soil made both diggers cough together, and Lara imagined the digging and the coughing would connect her to Maggs in a way that words had not. She found herself satisfied, smug even, that she was here digging, while Finley sat on a sunchair with his back to them, staring at the stars. And then, by turns, she felt ashamed. Because it was her, not Finley, who had killed the dog.

'You will become a doctor too, miss?' Maggs asked.

'I hope so,' Lara said. The stockman seemed unsatisfied by this, so she added, 'If I pass all my exams.'

'I think you'll pass easy, miss,' Maggs said. 'And a very fine doctor you'll make. Don't ask me how I know, it's just something in your aspect, miss, if you don't mind me saying. Oh please don't cry miss, I didn't mean to. . .'

Lara sat down, hugged her legs and wept. Finley hastened from his chair and knelt down on the dirt beside her, checking her pulse while he watched the pattern of her breathing. When their eyes met, he looked away. He returned to the sunchair and continued looking up at the Southern Cross.

She felt—though perhaps it was an illusion of light and mood—that there had been some genuine worry in his eyes. She found herself softening, the way she did when people around her unveiled their character, almost like a rule of thumb in her life. She looked at the doctor and the stockman and the dog, dead in its shroud, and she felt pained not just by its death but by all the things that its death had revealed.

'She's fine,' Finley said to Maggs, stretching his arms as he stood up from the sunchair. 'She's just not used to the country life. We'll show her how it's done, Maggs.'

Doctor and stockman took their shovels and dug, their frames silhouetted against the pasture, shovels rising and falling in sync, like a chain gang in an old movie, dirt flicking back behind black phantoms.

Lara heard the stockman muttering to himself as he dug. 'You saved my life. Saved my life, doctor. Dogs come and dogs go. Can't be bitter.' Like that he went on, driving the shovel into the dirt with greater force each time.

'It's done,' Maggs said at last, throwing the shovel on the floor and rubbing sweat off his neck with the back of his hand. Then he marched to where the dog lay in its towel shroud. He lifted it preciously and carried it to the hole and placed it inside.

A cool breeze brushed the back of Lara's neck. She held her breath as though half-expecting the dog to jump out of the hole and launch towards them. All three stared down the hole uneasily. Lara wondered if they were all seized by some version of her childlike idea—or hope or fear—of resurrection. But the white towel did not stir. Dead as an autopsy.

Afterwards, they washed their hands with a backyard hose and followed Maggs into his home. He had insisted they join him for dinner. The house was dim, its few scattered lightbulbs either broken or flickering madly, close to their end. Maggs brought out a tray of buttered white sandwiches with cheese, quartered neatly and served with black tea.

Lara scanned the room and saw artwork scattered randomly, some hung up, others leaning against the walls or even flush with the floor. Beaming when he noticed her interest, Maggs remarked that his real passion was mosaic work, which he constructed with eggshells and paint made from earthen pigments. His eyes danced as he spoke, and Lara was able, for a precious few moments, to forget why she was there. She listened to him describe how he chose his subject matter, prepared his materials, preserved the product.

'Preservation is the hardest part,' he said solemnly.

She tried to match the stockman's passion for his craft with her questions, and for a long time they spoke as though Finley was not there. She did not want to look at him, and noticed only his shadow fidgeting, the dress shoe tapping the squeaky floorboard erratically.

'We ought to get going,' he said. He sounded so tired then. He was older than he looked at the airport. 'You'll need to settle into your lodgings. Unpack. We've got an early start tomorrow.'

This time, it was the doctor who drove. He was sullen, and made sharp movements of the gearbox and exaggerated, unnecessary adjustments of his seat. He put the floodlights on. He didn't say a word.

One day she would ask him about his hobbies—she'd pick him for a stamp collector. Cars too, of course. But probably not a topic for today.

After she had unpacked her bags and lay in her bed, staring at the ceiling, she remembered the peculiar little things she'd noticed that strange night, but pushed aside. Shadows cast in the corner of her mind, less important than the real events. The way Finley had taken folds of cash from his wallet and placed them under a coaster on Maggs' dining table—to pay for what exactly? The way he looked away from her. It would be a long eight weeks.

A BACKYARD WEDDING

EILLISH BRENNAN

It is my sister's wedding, and I am sitting in a deck chair, head-on with the setting sun as it passes over the glowing bushland that served as the backdrop to where we all grew up. The light falls across the vast space, soft with a smile, watching absent-mindedly at the guests who dance with laughter across their faces and in the creases of their sweating skin. They clap their hands and tap their feet to the tunes that reverberate through the soil, into the spines of the worms that carry the movement forward through the earth and into the roots of the trees. The roots turn into the twisting trunks, and the branches with the gum leaves join in the dancing above all their bobbing heads. The beat of the bodhran—the sound of our ancestors—comes back to life in the stomping of the feet. And I watch on, an observer from my chair, but joined to the party all the same through my blood, which pulses in time with the collective beating of hearts. The magpies sing as backing for the band. There is harmony in everything now, a kind of cherished recognition of the presence of the moment. People look around at everyone that they have ever loved, or have seen in photos, or at events of the long-gone past. Some have gotten older, with grey in their hair, and wrinkles about their eyes. Some are leaning over more, a bit like the old estate that stands still in waiting behind the dancefloor, watching on. The estate with the weathered roof and sun-damaged bricks and the cobweb corners feels alive tonight, as if the ghosts could never have existed within its walls and writes them off as fantasy once and for all. For never has a place felt more concentrated with the breath of the living.

There is a glowing from the lights now as the infinite sky grows dark. There are pendants that glow amber, and tiny fairy bulbs that glitter like stars in everyone's eyes. There are coloured beams projected into the trees, who are grateful to be lit in recognition and revered. Against the glow, the soft darkness has crept in quietly and paints the guests in a camouflage of shadow. It has slowly covered the bodies so that the souls are all that's left behind. And they move more impassioned across the middle of the floor, deep into the night. There is a group of young men dancing together. I see them out of the corner of my eye. I've seen some of them before, perhaps, but mostly they are strangers. They're linking arms and laughing as they move across the grass to the music. They must be old friends laughing about something understood between only them. I think I must understand it too.

Tonight, watching on, I feel I might be beautiful. That is when he looks at me and smiles. He has noticed me, or perhaps he noticed me all night—was catching quiet glimpses of me out the corner of his eye. His eyes are blue and pierce through my skull. I hold his gaze longer than usual and return his smile. He feels familiar to look at. I wonder if I have looked at him before. I want to join the dancing, but instead, I walk to the bonfire that sits separate up the back, under the old Hills Hoist, now adorned in glowing light. There are other people standing and sitting around, watching the flames in a meditative circle. I think they are sharing in some kind of prayer. I sit myself beside the fire in an empty chair as the music and the laughter dance delicately about our heads. I watch as people chatter with smiles and searching eyes. There is curiosity amongst them and infinite things to be learned and known. I try to listen but can only make out the odd word here and there. The rest is drowned out by the cracking of the fire's flames. I hear the footsteps of someone behind me. They stop at my right and take a seat. It's the young man from the floor. He smiles again as I turn my head. The heat of the flames lick at my skin.

'Hi,' he says.

'Hi,' I reply with a smile.

'Is it alright if I join you?'

'Of course.'

From strangers to a collision of words and flesh, now undeniably familiar.

He asks me how I know the bride. I tell him that we share the same blood. He asks me if I am having a good night. I tell him I have never felt more alive. He asks me how I spend my time outside of this moment. I tell him about something that I do that maybe doesn't ignite my soul as much as moments like this, that maybe it was never something I felt I was fated to fulfil. But that it was good enough for now. That it got me where I wanted to be. He asks me where it was that I wanted to be. I think about home. I think about the wild sprawl that surrounds us and how I used to climb in the trees. I think about the old estate that watched me grow from child to adolescent. I think about how despite the passing of time—all the different cities and places in between—a part of me was always stuck sitting in that tree. *I don't tell him this.* I look at him and smile quietly. He smiles back. I tell him I'm not always sure I know what I want. He swigs his beer and nods in silence.

We look at the fire and listen. Now, we can hear the soft breeze that flows off the ocean and glides its way across the fields to meet the trees above our heads, bringing with it the scent of shells and seaweed. The gumnuts chime in with the rustle and shimmy of hibiscus. Someone lights up, and the fumes join paths with the smoke of the flames in front of our hot, red faces. I catch a glimpse of him in the fiery glow. He has stubble across his face that covers sun-worn skin like moss. I think he spends a lot of time outside. The type of person who loves to walk amongst the trees. The trees that never have to question why they are there or their purpose in the soil. He seems like he isn't someone that needs a watch. I ask him if he has the time. He says it's the best time of the night.

I am still at the fire, and my feet have turned black from the dirt. In the darkness, I can barely distinguish them from the ground. He hands me a glass of champagne. I am already a little drunk, but I accept it graciously. He asks me, 'What is the worst thing you have ever done?' A man on his right—hearing the question as directed at him—chimes in and tells us a story. I listen at some distance but am mostly watching the way the young man listens and drinks in the words of the stranger, beer in hand. Head down, he concentrates and smiles, imagining the little anecdote as it unravels before us in vague colours and distorted imagery. A story that only we can see in this moment, appearing out of the flames from a time gone by. Our eyes in sync widen at the climax, and we laugh as it all comes to an inevitable end. We laugh in appreciation for the collective memory that we now share. A sacred piece of history come back to life for an instant. He looks at me to see if I get it. I smile softly. There are stars now above our heads, some twinkling, some gently moving through space, some barely visible at all. One shoots past them all in a flash, and I am the only one who sees. I tell the others about it. They tell me to make a wish. I make a wish for everyone beneath its glow.

The young man has edged in closer to me. I didn't notice it happening, and I wonder if I had been the one moving closer the whole time. There is a part of me that wants to touch his knee with my own, or perhaps the space between his shoulder and arm where the skin is smooth and bare. Or even to accidently place my foot on top of his. I wonder if he would budge. I wonder if he would pull back. At one point, he laughs and leans into me. I burn at a brief flesh encounter.

I look back towards the dancefloor, still alive with guests. I see my sister in the centre in her whirling wedding dress, now dirtied at the hem. She is dancing with a smile, and her hair falls against her cheeks wildly like festive ribbons. Her husband is next to her, joining in the dance. The look of the deepest of love and excitement fills both their eyes and seeps into the hearts of everyone watching on. A sense of hope falls from the new lovers, heavy like honey, enrobing the guests in the sweetest of shared dreams. There is much revere on the dancefloor tonight. And by this fire. And under these stars.

I ask the man quietly what he thinks about love. He tells me about his most recent heartbreak. He tells me that he loved someone once, not too long ago. He tells me how they met, that they went to school together. He tells me how they stopped talking as they grew older, and their forms took different shape—comprised of different atoms. How they started to see each other less, forgot the feeling of each other's flesh kiss. He tells me how sometimes, when he is alone at night in bed, he remembers how her lips were the softest feeling in the world. I ask him if he minds being alone. He tells me he doesn't know. I ask him how he doesn't know. He takes a moment of silence, ritually swigs his beer, grips it in his fists, and then starts to say something but catches himself. He is looking at me, this man with piercing blue eyes and a dusting of stubble, and I think I understand his silence. He smiles at me. He tells me he doesn't feel alone tonight. I smile back, and we listen to the sounds of the guests and the wind off the sea and how it meets the trees and makes them shiver. I feel as though the words may have come from my own mouth.

He looks at me and puts down his beer—nearly empty. He stands and puts out his hand in offering. I look at it and back to him. He is asking me to dance. He smiles. I smile back and place my hand in his. Together, we make our way to the dancefloor, still filled with impassioned partygoers, and lovers and friends. He links arms with me in a dance and the rest of the party joins in. We laugh like children, moving through the crowd, sharing hands with one another, ducking under arching arms as the backyard band breaks into a jig. People are kicking their legs into the centre and clapping their hands with spirit. The young man's shadow and I dance across the floor, and I forget what it was that we had left unanswered.

The dancing has come to an end and the music has faded to a hum. The darkness has reached its peak, run swift across the sky with tarry black paint. But against it, the stars shine brighter still. People have staggered off in small groups, kissing each other with love and graciousness in their eyes as they depart from the scene. There are cans and cake and cheese scattered around the tables, signs of full stomachs and drunken lips. The grass that held up the dancing feet is worn and tired, yet the echoes of festivities still reverberate through it all like a resonant frequency. Some sit in chairs, mustering the energy to make their departure in a drunken haze and half-dream bliss. We walk back to the fire, some of the only few remaining. Perhaps this was the heart of it all—the burning furnace sustaining the movement and the hearts and the flesh. But even embers stop glowing given enough time. The tongues of the flames have lowered, plunging everyone into the darkness of shadow. It's harder to distinguish the night from the living. I feel him next to me though, sometimes warmer than fire. Some time passes as we watch the glow fade. Perhaps we secretly hope it never will. He says, 'I've always loved the way a fire knows when to stop burning.' The last of the laughter can be heard.

A possum in the tree above has perched itself close to the remains of the warmth. It watches the people below as they huddle and thinks lovingly about the tree that holds it above their heads.

Soon, it is just the young man and I, and a weak glow of amber amongst the ashen logs. We have grown tired of words. At one point, we found each other's hands in the darkness and held on. I felt the pulse of the evening again, echoed in his wrist. The young man leans in to kiss me, smelling of campfire and ash and beer. His chin is rough against my cheek, a bit like the bark beneath us. His mouth is warmer than bonfire. And I feel like I recognise him again. I feel like I know him through and through—have always known him. Despite words, despite stories, I feel a familiarity in the sharedness of our breath. There are mosquitos around our legs now, landing silently to feed their empty stomachs with the warmth of our blood. I am warm when he pulls away. The fire has turned black. I imagine we are the last burning embers that remain.

ALL THE PRETTY BIRDS

ALEXANDRA O'SULLIVAN

She was wearing the wrong dress. *Shit*. She knew the minute she saw the other girls that she'd got it all wrong. She knew, really, she knew when she bought the dress, but she'd had the confidence then of being on her own, of saying to herself, *I like this and it's not going to be quite like the others and that's fine because I like it. That's why I like it, actually.* And she'd just lost her head then, really, and bought the bag and those big sunglasses, and *shit*… the beret to go on her head. The red beret that she'd thought at the time made her look unique, stylish and European, but that she realised now just made her look pretentious.

But when she bought it, Naomi thought the beret was the cherry on top. She'd been so impressed by how she'd put it all together. That's what they were always saying about the fashions on the field winners. It wasn't just the dress, or the accessories they wore, it was how the dress and the accessories had been 'put together.' It gave the sense of being an artist, of creating yourself into something different by finding things and attaching them to your body in just the right way.

Naomi had never been invited to a marquee before. She'd been to the races before, but only as part of the general public, and she only went so she could gaze at the horses—exquisite creatures in the absolute prime of health, their coats glowing and their muscles rippling as they paraded by—it was never to glam up and parade herself. That's probably why she'd lost her head about the dress and everything. Chase had told her that the other girls were getting dressed up, and so, not wanting to look like she hadn't made an effort, she'd raced off to the shops and bought it all.

Now, as she lifted her new shoes over the grass towards the big, white tent, clutching Chase on the bicep while she positioned her sunglasses over her eyes with her other hand, she felt herself shrinking inside. She could see the other girls flashing across the entrance of the marquee. Bright, colourful birds with shiny, satin feathers, and vivid plumage on their glossy heads. Tripping about in their heels. Heels! She'd gone for flat sandals, European style to go with the dress and the hat and the sunglasses, but these girls all had heels on, stabbing into the grass as they walked.

When she got closer, she saw that the birds were actually more beautiful from a distance. Their shiny satin was really quite garish, and it was stretched uncomfortably over their breasts and stomachs. Their faces were slathered with orange paint and already shiny with sweat, and their heels were sticking their legs to the grass, so they moved like string puppets, making their fascinators shudder. Naomi, in her sensible sandals, loose cotton dress and flat beret wished she was wrapped in horrible satin with her heels sticking into the grass more than anything in the world.

They went through the entrance and Naomi fought the urge to rush at the drinks table. The white sheets of the tent were all around her.

'Glad you could make it.'

Chase's boss, Daniel, was standing in front of them. Naomi felt Chase's bicep flicker under her hand as he looked up to meet Daniel's eye. She lets her fingers slip off as she did the same. The horse trainer seemed taller now than when she'd seen him out at the stables. At his work he was always stooped over doing up girth straps, or, rushing, hunched forward, with a horse or two on a lead beside him. He'd give Naomi a smile on his way past, or he'd yell out that Chase was on his last horse, that he'd be with her soon. Sometimes he'd wink when he said it, but he'd always be gone before Naomi could think how to respond.

'You know Naomi,' Chase was saying now, giving her a rough pat on the shoulder as introduction.

'Of course,' he said, grazing his eyes across her. 'You look nice,' he added, as an afterthought.

Naomi smiled faintly and lifted her sunglasses from her eyes.

'The girls are around,' Daniel continued, waving his hand vaguely. 'You know the girls, don't you, Naomi?'

'Yes.'

Naomi had seen the girls, too, whenever she picked Chase up at the stables, but they looked different to the ones she saw now. At the stables, they wore muddy jeans or tattered track pants, thick-soled work boots, and stained T-shirts. They had their hair scrunched back. They moved fluidly between horses to run confident hands over them in a way that made Naomi suck in her breath. Now, they stumbled around the marquee, laughing as champagne sloshed out of their plastic glasses. Naomi focused on a plain-looking girl who was wearing an orange-coloured dress with a V-shape at the back that had seams digging into her shoulder blades, like it was cut to be in direct conflict with her body, like she had to fight to wear it. A yellow fascinator, like a strange growth, stuck out the side of her head.

'Tangerine dream,' she whispered in Chase's ear.

'Naomi, don't be mean,' he whispered back, laughing all the same. 'We can't all be gorgeous like you,' he added, making Naomi regret her cruelty.

'Well, help yourselves to food and drink' Daniel said before he moved away to greet the next guests who were just arriving.

She dragged Chase by the arm towards the drinks table, selected a tall glass of champagne and tipped most of it down her throat. 'They're off!' Echoed in the distance, followed by the indecipherable gabble of the caller. The first race was underway. On the other side of the tent a girl turned and started waving excitedly. Naomi stared, then realised that she was waving at Chase, not her. Naomi drained her glass as the girl came towards them, then stood holding it, empty, as the girl launched straight into a retelling of the horse that morning who'd bit Chase 'right on the arse.'

'How's his bruise going?' She asked Naomi, grinning.

'She'll tell you tomorrow,' Chase replied.

Their laughter was too loud for how close they were standing together. It bounced around the marquee and brought more people towards them. Above it, the race call reached a crescendo.

There were far more women than men, Naomi noticed, and it was three girls who now stood, adjusting their satin dresses, and chatting to Chase, while Naomi gripped his sleeve and stared at her refilled champagne glass.

'Naomi, isn't it?' She was being asked by a long-legged blonde wearing a bright purple dress that reminded Naomi of her school formal five years ago, a lifetime ago.

'Yes.'

'I'm Sasha,' she replied. 'You look nice, that beret is cute, so foreign.'

'Yeah, you should go in fashions,' the bland-faced girl beside her said.

Naomi couldn't work out if she meant it seriously or was having a private joke.

Tangerine dream, she thought, and felt better. She put her empty champagne glass down and picked up a full one.

'Isn't it great of Daniel to get us a whole marquee!' Sasha continued. 'The races are so much better when you have a marquee.'

'Yeah, he's a champ,' Chase agreed. 'Much better than last year's Christmas party!'

'Oh my God!' Sasha burst into giggles. 'At that old winery! And you disappeared down the vines with...' she trailed off, glanced quickly at Naomi. 'You disappeared,' she finished lamely.

Chase grinned. 'Yeah, I guess it was pretty fun after all.'

Naomi hadn't known Chase when he was at the Christmas party last year. When he was disappearing down the vines. They'd met only six months ago at the races. She'd been leaning against the rail of the parade ring, her eyes glued on the horses, gorging on the rippling muscles and glossy coats. Their angular faces. Their dark eyes like lakes.

'You like horses, hey?'

She'd looked sideways to see a man standing beside her. He wasn't very tall, but he'd looked at her as if from a great height. He had brown, gold-flecked eyes and a hint of laughter dancing across the rugged contours of his face.

'Yes.'

'I'm a track rider, number five, that's the one I ride.'

He'd pointed out a dark bay who was jogging up and down as if on springs, throwing its rump this way and that, while the wisp of a girl at the lead dug her heels into the ground and clanked the bit in his mouth, trying to anchor the horse to her.

'Wow, that's so cool!'

'I could show you the stables sometime.'

And he had done just that. The smell of the horses was stronger at the stables than at the races. It was mixed with the smell of hay and shit and piss that seemed to make it more real; it wasn't diluted by the perfumes of the people jammed beside her, by the fresh grass and the flowers by the parade ring. At the stables, Naomi didn't have to just stand there and look at the horses, she could go up the stable doors. She could touch them on the nose. Chase was happy to tell her which ones wouldn't bite her. He'd come up and stand beside her, lean casually against the door, and let the horse push her head against his shoulder. He'd reach his hand up to scratch his fingers beneath the forelock, making the horse squint her eyes with pleasure.

Another race call brought Naomi back to the present. How many races had run? She had no idea. She moved towards the marquee entrance, pulled her sunglasses down against the glare, and watched the race crowd moving across the lawn: men and women in their immaculate race clothes, some with race books and some with newspapers folded back to the form guide. They were like characters in a painting, each figure complimenting the entire scene, an artist's creation of a day at the races.

I could show you the stables sometime. What was it he was really showing her, leaning against the door the way he did? Scratching his fingers under the forelock?

'Are you having a nice time?'

Naomi turned to see a small, sweet-faced girl looking up at her. She held a glass of champagne as if she didn't really know what it was for. She didn't look old enough to drink.

'Yes, thank you.'

'You're Chase's girlfriend, right?'

'Yes,' she replied, then added, as an afterthought, 'Naomi.'

'He's such a good rider, we're all so impressed with his riding. He's taught me heaps.

He's so good with the horses, the way he can just talk them into anything.' The girl sighed dreamily. 'Are you a rider too?' She looked up at Naomi eagerly.

'No, I don't ride, I love horses though.'

Naomi couldn't explain that she didn't see the point of riding, of trying to control all that beauty and power. You could see horses much better when you weren't riding them.

'So, you follow the races, then? You like to bet?'

'Not really, I just… admire the horses'

'Oh, okay.'

The girl swirled her drink, carefully watching as it circled her glass, her biceps, big for such a small girl, flexed beneath the frilled sleeves of her dress.

Beautiful, aren't they? She could have said, or, *Yes, I know what you mean.* But she didn't, so they had nothing left to say. Naomi sipped her champagne and looked away. She saw Chase on the other side of the marquee, now sitting on one of the white, plastic chairs. Tangerine dream was sitting on his lap, pressing her bum into his crotch and he was laughing. He liked all this, she realised. He didn't find any of it ridiculous, he enjoyed it all.

'Sorry Naomi, I've stolen your man,' Tangerine dream called across the tent.

She tipped back her head and let out a short, high-pitched laugh, pressing her head growth into Chase's grinning face.

'You can have him.'

It came out more bitter than she expected. It was supposed to be a light-hearted joke—something to show she was totally cool with it all, just like them, fun and up for a laugh. But it didn't land that way. There was an awkward silence. Then Naomi forced a laugh through her throat, but it was too late. She filled her mouth with champagne.

They'd been put together all wrong. It was her mistake. No matter how she put herself together, it would never be in a way he would appreciate. She wasn't one of the bright birds.

She was dark feathered, with little specs of secret colour hidden beneath her wings. He would never see it. It wasn't her fault she didn't want to lift her wings up and show him; he was too easily dazzled by the light that already surrounded him. He didn't want to go searching for it. *Searching down in the vines*, Naomi thought, her head spinning.

It was only later, when they were leaving, Naomi gripping his sleeve and tripping in her European sandals, her beret sliding off her head, that she realised, she hadn't seen a horse all day.

GENGHIS KHAN

G.M. MONKS

I've seen them before. Fifty, seventy,
maybe two hundred chumming around
like a family reunion in a favorite park.
        Then they might've been hunting,
    figuring out what to do next in the warm
        spring sun. Smelling the air.
            Where's the food?
        What's the quickest way to get it? I walked
            into them but they saw or smelled me and made
way. I passed by, then turned around. They were
    back at it, never caring who I was,
        be it god or a peon or a mirage.

            Coming back, I saw them again
                on a path near a slippery elm tree
            by a noisy creek, in the shade
                    speckled with sunlight.
                Could've been another favorite
            hangout. I wondered if some wanted
                romance, making plans. They didn't notice me.
        I was drawn towards them. The little spots of life
    silently fluttered all different ways, like a
            sphere reshaping itself and disappearing
    in welcoming shadows.

In truth, I was plain rude, walking into their party,
            uninvited, like Genghis Khan invading the Steppes.
But they acquiesced having better things to do
        than squabble with a nuisance, if I was even noticed.
            They flirted, shared aromas, or chased one another
                or whatever they were doing
                in their quiet gnat universe.

4
MOONLIGHT

LAVATIME

ALICE GORMAN

Waking up on the Moon was a process of adjustment. Sleep was such a terrestrial phenomenon, she had decided. In the transition before her eyes opened, she always felt herself to be still 'at home', in the Earth bedroom, the Earth bed with the pale green satin quilt that no longer existed. It was a moment of disorientation before she became fully conscious of where she was.

The residues of bright trees fled from her dreams. She could set her room's 'window' to show any view she liked from Earth—such earthly connections were held to be beneficial for the mental health of the lunarians—but somehow these digital forests seemed less real than the trees formed solely inside her sleeping brain. Hers were usually eucalypts with long glossy leaves and piebald cream-and-brown trunks. Sometimes the hum of insects hung in the leaves, barely leaving an imprint in her mind as the regular morning sounds of the lunar habitat started to overwrite them.

So she did not usually turn the window on to Earth. She preferred the live feed to the surface. Not many of her colleagues did; but somehow this made the Moon real for her, stabilising her here. The unchanging, silent, grey surface was an anchor to a reality that grew further and further away from Earth the longer she stayed.

The surface was never as still or boring as the others believed though. Over the 15 Earth days of lunar sunlight, the angle of the light slowly changed, and she saw the plain, strewn with rough boulders, reveal different contours and textures to her gaze. It was quite dynamic, really, if snail-slow in its progress sometimes. Time was such a moveable feast on the Moon. Inside the lava tube, they worked to a local clock which matched circadian rhythms, aided by artificial light and dark; they communicated with Earth using Coordinated Universal Time; and they pitted themselves against the implacable force of the long lunar day, which would have frozen them in its dawn and boiled them at its noon. Of the lunar night they did not speak.

When she arrived, one of the first cohort of people to inhabit the Murasaki lava tube, her primary visual referent for the lunar landscape was images from the 1960s. US astronauts had spent a combined 58 hours on the surface at six locations, such a tiny sample of the Moon's variety, but the pictures were still imprinted on the global consciousness. They were like an early silent movie;

very like, in fact, the black-and-white French film of a voyage to the Moon made even earlier that century, populated by comical characters in highly impractical costumes. Her personal experience had long since replaced the proxies offered by the first generation of astronauts. She had her own iconography of the lunarscape now.

The surface feed was piped into the habitat by a static camera facing outwards from the skylight gate. The camera also collected data on lunar weather. It faced across the grey plain, with the vista truncated in the distance by mountains which cast shadows like teeth. About 40 km in the opposite direction there was a Chinese lava tube habitat. Even further away was a private habitat established by the MoonCorp mining consortium.

Over breakfast, cereal and coffee made in her kitchenette, she watched the light inch across her favourite rock. She was a geologist by training, so she was allowed to have favourite rocks. This one appealed to her for two reasons. For a portion of lunar day, the shadows cast by indentations in the rock's surface coalesced to form a face, a rather friendly one with a look that seemed to say, 'How are you today? Just checking in from my place out here'. As the light moved, the face's smile broadened and then narrowed, just a little sadly, and the 'eyes' appeared to look at something beyond her field of view. The smile lasted about four days of lavatime. Pareidolia was such a human impulse, such an intuitive way of bringing meaning to the incomprehensible.

At another time of lunar day, a row of parallel striations was visible on the rock. If she had seen them on Earth, she'd have attributed them to a glacier scraping along its surface. Here, their cause was mysterious. This rock had had a journey; it had a history of its own.

Her favourite rock was a watching thing, keeping vigil while she slept. At night, it was swallowed up in darkness. It could have been doing anything: leaping up on spidery legs and going to visit other rocks; scampering up to the camera to pull faces that would not be recorded. Just as the Earth night harboured all humanity's fears and doubts, so too the lunar night masked the unknown terrors of the Moon. No-one knew what the antidotes were out here, what rituals and talismans to use against the dark. No-one knew what monstrosities hid in the iced deeps. No-one watched the night. Inside the tube they tuned their windows to yellow beaches, gardens bursting with flowers, or the city streets where they used to live, until they switched them off for sleep.

But she kept the surface feed going through the fortnight of darkness. Someone had to watch her rock, even if it were invisible, as if they had a pact which guaranteed each other's existence. And besides, at night the stars shone more brilliantly, and you had a grand view of the frequent meteorites. A couple more weeks and they'd be passing through the Eta Aquariid meteor shower, icy fragments thrown off by Halley's Comet. No waiting for a lucky glimpse of a falling star: on the Moon you could have wishes every day.

After wiping her dishes clean, she threw off her pyjamas and applied the same process to her own body; then she put on work clothes and went into the corridor. Here, the corridors were streets. Residents were milling about, chatting before heading off in different directions to their offices and laboratories. She waved to a couple of neighbours, with whom she shared the occasional wine after work.

Her job was operating and monitoring a network of seismic instruments, using the remote sensing data they gathered to build virtual models of the lava tube network. Of course this could have been done just as well from Earth, but there had to be some work for the lunarians to do. They weren't here for a holiday. At the moment she had a dinky little rover mapping the lava tube beyond the habitat. They were hoping for a long, unbroken tunnel that could be used to extend the habitat, and provide transport to a known KREEP area rich with rare Earth elements. Travelling underground was so much safer than the surface.

The Lunar Observations department was a 15-minute walk from her apartment. While she could work from home, it was also held to benefit the well-being of the lunarians to be social; to share ideas; to form micro-communities. And they were right, she thought, even though the selection criteria for the lunarian workforce didn't weed out the mansplainers. There was still a gender imbalance in the small off-planet populations. Some things took a long time to change.

In the office she went straight to her workstation. First, she checked the seismometers. These were located in various places around the plain within a radius of about 20 km, as well as inside the Murasaki tube. They kept tabs on the structural stability of the tube, which was assaulted by deep quakes from below, and celestial impacts from above. All was quiet. Overnight there had been no moonquakes, meteor strikes, or space junk crashing onto the Moon. The instruments also picked up rocket launches and landings, but as the schedules were pre-circulated among all the lava tube habitats, there was usually little to cause surprise.

Then she logged into the rover. The data download continued overnight so there was a new section of the lava tube, over two kilometres wide, to process and calibrate against the orbital data. The rover managed an average of one kilometre a day on its sticky feet, scanning the walls with its lasers to build up a detailed 3D image of a rough-walled tunnel with dendritic off-shoots. Two billion years ago, when the magma pulsed under the Moon's skin, it chose the path of least resistance to burst onto the surface. There were many branches and dead ends that the orbital survey did not detect. The rover detoured to map these where it could, making the process a slow one. Sometimes it got stuck, and she had to manoeuvre it out. There were a couple of earlier rover corpses in the tunnel.

A week in lavatime passed without incident, except for an increase in meteors on the surface as the Moon drew closer to the main Eta Aquariid swarm. The map slowly built up, increment upon increment, until the day that the terminator, the edge of day, passed over them and plunged them into night.

As she sat at her desk, watching the layers of the lava tube slowly accrete on her screen, her eyes were arrested by a small geometric anomaly on the tunnel wall.

Of course it was easy to succumb to pareidolia, seeing patterns that weren't there, as she knew too well. She honed in on it. It wasn't a natural feature. It was the size and shape of a seismometer, the kind you bought off the shelf on Earth, similar to those deployed all around Murasaki. But it wasn't one of hers. Someone had already been down this tunnel, from the other end, and planted it.

The longest intact lava tubes they'd mapped from orbit were about 60 km. If this one were in that order of length, it might connect to the Chinese habitat.

Could this be true? Did the Chinese already know their tube connected with Murasaki? It would break every protocol to secretly monitor someone else's zone of operation, but now she wondered if she had missed the signs before. Everything was peaceful on the Moon, but there was no pretending it was any kind of utopia. The US and China had been weaponizing science to gain the upper hand on the Moon since the 2030s. They all knew the score. Even if you stayed non-aligned, like the Asia-Pacific consortium which managed Murasaki, there were stakes.

What was the end game? A covert assault on Murasaki, depressurising the habitat and killing all inside, leaving it empty for occupation? Who was going to do the forensics on that? An uneasiness started to thread itself through her veins.

She wrote a quick report and emailed it to her supervisor, copying in Murasaki headquarters in Tokyo. There was a short, perfunctory reply thanking her for the intelligence. This made her think that they weren't completely surprised. Well, it wasn't her place to interfere in international relations. Let the higher-ups deal with that.

The remaining hours of the workday wore away slowly as she processed the data. There were no more anomalies, and no further emails. She couldn't bring herself to mention the anomaly to her workmates; there were too many conspiracy theories about the Moon as it was. Back in her apartment, she declined an invitation to dine in the hall and then retire to one of Murasaki's bars. She made a small collation of cheese, biscuits, and dried fruit, and allowed herself a glass of Rutherglen port that she'd packed in her personal allowance. The unknown seismometer throbbed in her brain. She was in the dark about the consequences of her discovery.

When she finally got to sleep, she did not dream of the trees. Instead she was running through the tunnel from something nameless tracking her in the lunar night, something older than Earth.

She woke with a start, immediately alert. An instinct made her get up and open her computer to the seismic data. Just before midnight in lavatime, the sensors on the perimeter had registered vibrations which increased slowly in strength. This could have been something far away growing in intensity, or something of constant intensity drawing closer. It was not the signature of a moonquake or meteor strike.

It was now 1.00 am. Turning on her window to the surface feed, she saw something alarming. There were no scheduled surface missions, but there were moving lights in the otherwise stygian darkness. As they grew closer, she felt the vibration even without the aid of the seismometers, a trembling through the walls of the lava tube. Something heavy enough to disturb the regolith was approaching across the plain.

For the first time, she saw her favourite rock in the night. The vehicle's lights illuminated its hollows, but the kindly smile she usually saw from her window was a distorted mask. Her scientist's brain noted an extension of the striations which she hadn't seen before in natural light. Then the ridged caterpillar track crunched over her rock and shivered it into pieces.

A klaxon sounded inside the lava tube.

On the computer screen, her rover's data feed winked out. There was something in the tunnel. They were trapped from both sides.

Murasaki's external floodlights suddenly ignited, and she could see the encroaching vehicle. It was not like anything she had seen on the Moon before. It was a troop carrier, a behemoth, a Trojan Horse, fortified against the unearthly cold of the lunar night. Surely, no-one had known the Chinese were assembling such vehicles on the Moon.

But the floodlights also lit up the logo on the side of the vehicle. They weren't hiding their identity. The letters could just be made out through a thick coating of dust: 'MoonCorp LLC.' It wasn't the Chinese. If other vehicles were coming up the tunnel, then the Chinese habitat had already fallen. It was a hostile corporate takeover, an insolent gesture sullying the neutrality of the dark. Four billion years of a peaceful Moon had been broken in a matter of hours. She had no doubt they were already cut off from communications with Earth.

A meteor streaked through the black sky above the plain and then another.

The first night after the invasion, as uniformed MoonCorp mercenaries patrolled the corridors, and the Eta Aquariids bombarded the defenceless surface, she dreamt of her favourite rock, its friendly smile shattered, and its secret history crushed. Her allegiance was cast. She would resist and defend the vision of the Moon that was hers.

MOONLIGHT/STARLIGHT

EZ KNILL

god i'm hungry for the abstract / and i want to read everything i can get my hands on / hey, maybe i can one day write that which i wish to consume so bodily. / and oh! oh! sorry you had to be loved / by a poet, loved by me. / i promise i'm being so cool right now / don't even question it. / didn't you know i was made for the epilogue? / i don't think i have the stomach for the rest of it, / how do i explain it, then? it's like / i'm living in occupied space. / like i am the last guest entering an art museum / ten minutes before close, so sure that i'm going to be able to see everything on offer. / but i can't do that, can i?

no one can / look through all twenty rooms of my life / in the space of three songs and some change. / there are too many paintings by far, / too many portraits of memories / all by artists

i've not even heard of. / but it's me in all the paintings, isn't it? / yeah, you can see. that's me, right there on the wall. / i'm strung up for you all. / i'm yours to witness and analyse and critique. / the brush strokes here are too visible, / and there is so much colour / but not enough purpose. / god, it's funny, isn't it? / i'm every painting in the whole damn gallery— / that's my face / staring back from out the canvas and wood and pigment. / it belongs to me. i own it, / i hold it with a tenuous sort of reverence. / it's all me, all the way down— / and even still, i don't recognise myself.

not for all the first room / (one, two minutes gone) / all the second room / (a minute gone, to just the transition from room to room) / room three feels bigger than the other two by miles / (i lose a minute and another to staring up at the canvas stretched across the entire back wall. it's infallible in its enormity. it's me and not.) / how could i not see me? / how, when i sat for each one, / each pose my own long lines / of flesh and bone and sinew / room four / (two minutes) / much of these half-familiar reliefs, feel like memory coated in dust.

is it simply that i am every star bursting / too hot, too cold, too hard to understand? / i am the artist statement with no name, / i am the expectation and the creation, / not the created, not the creator. / i am in every room of this gallery / closing in three minutes. / how do i explain it, then? / how about this. i'm better off / in the moonlight starlight. / i look better in the night./ not so many spotlights / ground up, top down, light up every surface. / this is no place for shadow, / no place for me, / no place for what i know best. / this is no explanation, there is no answer here / no written statement of 'you' 'me' 'you.' / still, i'm spellbound by the paint and canvas of me / (not me). / so I bundle up coat and bag and map, / it's time to leave this mirrored gallery. / it's time to turn blind side to this look of me i've never seen before / and hope that no sketch of this too ends up nailed to the wall. / i am no painting / i am no artist / I am just living in this body like everyone else.

THE LEGACY OF SHADOWS

ADRIAN DOWNES

Ayan felt that it was going to be a good day. He stood and touched his fingertips against the window. Despite being triple glazed and toughened anticyclonic glass, the pane was warm from radiant heat trapped by the semi-toxic atmosphere that enveloped the planet. Since the Year of Darkness resulting from the Great Burn at the end of the War of Turmoil any change in seasons were barely discernible. The atmospheric balance had been destroyed in just under five years, and now there was little respite from the searing winds that swept the terrain.

But today despite the early hour there was a glimmer of a sunrise, streaking through the red miasma of smog. He traced its line on the glass and noticed his reflection, outlined by sunlight, the square features and the blunt mouth. The light struck faint shadows across the ground from the wind turbines. A few charred trees remained, and the hulk of the scrapped Icarus-X transporter rusting and being slowly consumed by drifting sand. Every day, the sun seemed a little stronger, as if battling the shadows on a daily basis.

Ayan checked the display module embedded into his left forearm and the monotone inflection of INTI his personal computer interface relayed appointments for the day via his audio implant.

INTI: <<Meeting 01 – 9.15am with Ereba Shamir Facility-8 Tea House.>>

He enjoyed his time with Ereba. She had grown and opened up immensely since she had arrived on the Icarus-X eighteen months ago as a refugee from the dark side of the planet following the War of Turmoil. Ayan's job as a Socio-facilitator had been to instruct her in the ways of the New Society; indoctrinate her in its social structure; help her attain the accreditation goals to become a True Citizen; and most importantly teach her how to survive the Climatic conditions. He had assisted her in finding a job, and with her scientific knowledge, she had proven quite dextrous at growing the plants and vegetable that sustained this community, working in the largest Hydro-dome. The domes dotted the landscape, and since the Year of Darkness, their glazed structures were heavily supplemented by Synthetic Daylight and each cast a violet glow onto the deep red smog clouds.

He inhaled a caffeine shot and pulled on his body suit. He didn't intend to venture outside so the full Hazmat was not required, but this suit still incorporated some environmental control systems.

INTI: <<Suit fully functioning, checks complete, no current hazards.>>

Ayan left the three-room apartment in Central-1 Tower. The unit was generous befitting his recently promoted status and much better than his initial subterranean accommodation. He touched the implant against a sensor panel and activated the elevator. He sped down fifty-eight floors, eight of them underground. These housed the Central administration facilities, retail marts, Casino and bars and certified brothels. Some reclassed workers and refugees still had dormitories here, but Ereba had recently been relocated to Facility-8, close to the Hydro-dome where she worked.

He took the Express Loop train, clutching the handrail as the carriage rattled at high speed through the tunnel. Emerging by travelator, his implant registered the cost of the journey as he passed the exit stile. He glanced up through the vast glass dome that had provided natural daylight when this had been a major shopping centre. Through the sand riven glass, the concrete hulk of Facility-8 loomed, silhouetted against the sky it's surface still blackened from the Great Burn.

INTI: <<Take the west mall, turn left at Chemoland, Tea House twenty metres on the right. You will arrive eight minutes early.>>

He hadn't been to this section of the Facility before and it was dirty and drab—mostly empty shopfronts and a few stalls selling repurposed plastic items and electronics. The Tea House wasn't much more appealing, brightly lit and starkly furnished, he was aware of a layer of dust on all the surfaces. He positioned himself in a small corner booth. Ereba had suggested this place, and it was her day off, so he had felt obliged to meet her here rather than at Central. 'What would you like, or do you need a menu?' The Waiter-Bot asked as it floated up to his table, its sensors blinking expectantly.

'Earl Grey tea, with lemon, no sugar please.'

INTI: <<Don't forget to hydrate today.>>

'Oh, and some tap water please' he added.

He spotted Ereba as she walked towards the Tea House. She nodded familiarly at a few of the stall keepers. Her blonde hair was tucked into a beanie but still marked her as not from this side of the planet. Her pale, almost translucent skin and piercing blue eyes set her apart from the Indigenous people of the Bright side, she appeared delicate and slight, almost glowing.

His own complexion was swarthy in comparison, his carbon black eyes and equally dark hair, today tied back. Ereba smiled and sat down at the table facing him.

'Hello Ayan, lovely to see you.' She still spoke with a stilted lilt as if reading from a prompter.

'Hi Ereba, what would you like to drink?' Ayan asked as the Waiter-Bot hovered.

'A Yuzu Soda please, no ice, thanks,' she spoke directly to the robot. 'I grow the Yuzu,' she said looking at Ayan.

INTI scanned Ereba's ID chip via Ayan's retinal implant and conveyed the results to his brain. Ereba being of a lesser class didn't have the full personal computer implant, instead a basic chip, and she had to use a simple fob for travel, credit and door entry which limited her movement throughout the Facility and the community in general.

INTI: <<Ereba Shamir 28, D-Class landscape operative, vital signs good, heart rate slightly irregular.>>

Ayan studied her, she seemed slightly agitated, touching the scars on her wrists. He felt a pang of guilt. She had been bound and interrogated when she had first arrived, a suspected terrorist or spy. Her father and sister had been known insurgents on the dark side of the planet and had been strategic in an attempt to undermine New Society in the War of Turmoil, a war which had escalated quickly over mineral exploration on the boundaries of the dark side of the planet. It had taken several months to determine her innocence, and she was broken and had self-harmed whilst incarcerated. Ayan slowly had to gain her trust and help mould her to become a valued citizen of the community. He had grown fonder of her than he cared to admit to INTI.

The Waiter-Bot brought their drinks, its mechanical arms carefully manoeuvring the cup and glasses onto the table. Ayan waved his arm across the sensor screen and the payment was recorded.

'How are you Ereba?' Ayan asked her.

She looked down at her soda, 'I haven't been sleeping well, I keep having a recurring nightmare about my family in The Burn. I tried to contact them multiple times once the war was over.'

Ayan knew the likelihood of any of them having survived was very slight.

'I have a twin brother, Pollo you know.' She sat forward a little.

He looked surprised; he hadn't known this. His thought query activated INTI.

INTI: <<There is no record of Pollo Shamir, dead or alive.>>

'Have you heard from him at all, since you arrived here?' He asked.

'He was supposed to be on the same transporter but didn't show up. I did receive an encrypted message when I arrived here but couldn't decode it and the authorities deleted it.'

She looked at him directly, the intense eyes as if probing him for information.

'Perhaps he might still be alive, I could do some digging across the Admin records,' he didn't want to pass on INTI's brutal message. Ereba sipped her soda. 'What about your family?'

They had never spoken about this, and Ayan was not supposed to discuss personal matters with others below his clearance level.

INTI: <<*Consider your next statements carefully.*>>

He ignored the computer. 'They all died in The Burn. I only survived as I was at the Academy. Everything I had known was destroyed; I was seventeen and was moved permanently into a dormitory. My new family of sorts.' He ran a finger wistfully around the rim of his cup.

'I'm sorry.' Ereba said. 'Everyone needs a family and some sort of legacy.'

His vision was attracted by a vividly bright video screen set into the grey tiled wall, advising citizens of a new vigilance level. Dissidents, even this long after the War of Turmoil still occasionally operated some terrorist cells attempting to disrupt the fabric of New Society, despite no known organised leadership existing.

Ayan tried to lighten the mood, 'Have you noticed the Sun?' he asked. 'Everyday it seems slightly stronger as if burning away the dust.'

'It does seem lighter in the Hydro-Dome some mornings,' she replied. 'But I grew up on the dark side, so I'm not used to the sun,' she laughed. 'I think I would combust if I went outside into full sunlight.' She gently touched the skin of her arm. 'We pale-skins always stand in your shadows and have for centuries.' Her eyes glistened as she smiled.

Ayan laughed and suddenly felt more relaxed. He wondered if she was attracted to him in any way and how it would be to hold her delicate body. He longed for intimacy, his last visits to the Brothel had been soulless and mechanical, and he had left feeling hollow. Relationships were generally frowned on, other than for reproduction and only then between approved classes as INTI reminded him.

INTI: <<*Relations between mismatched classes cannot be authorised.*>>

She reached across the table and touched his wrist which jolted him out of his thoughts.

'I would like to show you something I have been working on if you had time, my home unit is only a few minutes away,' she said.

He was intrigued, was this an invitation for something more than friendship?

INTI: <<Your next meeting is in sixty-seven minutes at Central.>>

'I only have a short time; what do you want to show me?' He asked.

'You'll see if you come; it won't take long.' She stood up and started to walk away, again acknowledging the stall keepers.

He followed her feeling both excited and reticent as she led him through a maze of laneways, up several flights of stairs to a front door identical to forty others lining the length of a poorly lit corridor.

INTI: <<This course of action is inadvisable, exercise caution.>>

Ereba touched the fob to the entry panel and pushed open the steel door. The interior was surprisingly bright despite only having a single small square window. A bed was pushed against one wall draped with a multicoloured blanket, the kitchen module was clean and tidy. A framed picture of sunflowers hung on one wall, next to a screen displaying current news content. Ayan then noticed a console table against the opposite wall littered with electrical components and cables, lithium batteries, small metal components. Several heavy plastic containers were stacked underneath.

'Is this what you wanted to show me Ereba? What are you making?' He asked.

'Sit down, Ayan, let me show you.'

He sat on a hard chair between the bed and the console and was inspecting the elements when he was suddenly aware of another person who had stepped silently from the darkness of the bathroom into the living space. Ayan turned and, for a moment, thought he recognised this man; the facial features and gait were familiar to him. INTI scanned the stranger.

INTI: << Alexis Fordham 27, D-Class Chemical-Cleaning operative. Origin unknown.>>

It became clear to him, it was Ereba's face, with one side heavily scarred by a burn. He had the same eyes and nose, the same curved lips, but shrouded by a beard and thick black hair. Ayan turned to Ereba confused and then studied the console table again.

INTI: << Potential bomb components, exit immediately.>>

'Ayan, this is my twin, Pollo or Alexis as he is known now. I told you about him; he did make it here alive and we are working together now.'

Ayan stood suddenly, as Alexis swung a heavy metal rod he had concealed behind his back. Ayan was struck on the side of the head and slumped heavily onto the vinyl floor.

INTI: << Temporary cerebral shutdown.>>

Ayan regained consciousness, confused as to where he was or how long he had been sitting. He tried to flex but was tightly bound to the chair with plastics ties that cut into his skin.

Golden light danced across the bed from the small window. His head throbbed and he was aware of an intense pain in his left forearm. Glancing down, he saw his arm was crudely bandaged with heavily blood-stained gauze. Two fine wires jutted from the top edge of the bandage—the remnant connections of his interface module. There was a pool of congealed blood around his feet. He summoned INTI but there was no response.

INTI: <<<<<<<<<< >>>>>>>>>>>

His mind felt empty and quiet without electrical impulses constantly being transmitted. He tried to remember the day and date but without INTI supplementing knowledge he felt blank.

He raised his aching head and looked at the wall screen display. Live images were being shown of a firestorm in the largest Hydro-Dome, video footage relayed a blinding flash and then the huge structure partially collapsed. Scrolling news text at the bottom of the screen referred to suicide bombers and multiple bombs having been detonated.

<<Half of the Community's fresh food sources destroyed.>>

The images changed to the exterior of Central with clouds of smoke billowing from shattered windows.

<< A suicide bomber gained access to high security tunnels below the electro-chemical storage at Central. Investigations underway. Partial collapse of the Facility imminent. Emergency crews in attendance. Dozens killed.>>

Images of Ereba and Alexis from their Admin ID files flashed onto the screen—the close resemblance of the two was blatantly clear to Ayan. Further text scrolled across the screen.

<<ID chips have identified two of the accused bombers. Senior Socio-

Facilitator Ayan Carman of Central also implicated in the security breach; whereabouts currently unknown.>>

Additional faces appeared on the screen, several of the stall holders from Facility-8 and then Ayan's headshot was displayed; looking corporate and professional, he stood in front of a large group of refugees, pre-processing. They are crouched on the floor, only one or two smiling at the camera; Ereba, pale and thin, stares directly into the lens at the far right of the image.

The daylight in the apartment faded and the room became swathed in deep shadow. Wind lashed sand across the window, twinkling black and gold as flames flickered from the burning Hydro-Dome. Ayan's head nodded, and he slipped into unconsciousness.

5
ELECTRIC LIGHT
SMOKE
& MIRRORS

IN WHICH A SOCKED FOOT, A CAT, TWO AVOCADOES AND A GODDESS TAKE FLIGHT, AND COUNT LEO TAKES A BOW

SCOTT WINKLER

PROLOGUE

Laura and Adam lived together in a small serviceable flat on the east side. They got along on almost everything; films, museums, most TV shows and on politics they both leaned left, she more than him. They bought stuff to eat, cooked together and usually they ate together, except when Adam fussed over his work, then they ate separately. Like tonight, Adam at his computer in his work nook and Laura on her phone in the dining room texting and messaging everyone she knows with one hand while eating with the other, her legs curled up under her and one foot sticking out. Adam can see her socked foot and above it the pretzel formation of her legs but not her upper body. From the waist up she is cut off by the doorway and short hallway between them. A bright light hangs in the kitchen behind her, a single high-watt bulb covered by a cheap plexiglass cover from the 1980s or 90s. This back-light projects into Adam's work nook the various textures, colors, curls and lengths of Laura's lower body as silhouetted blacks, browns and grays. The prominent socked foot stares at him sideways while bobbing up down and around in some sort of early 21st century tribal rhythm.

Laura worked with the elderly in their last years, not an easy job but it had its rewards and it didn't come home with her like his work. Still, Adam pleased her. She might have loved him, she thought she did. He seemed different from the others. There was a gentleness. He wasn't so blatantly manly, so testoseroney. They had lived together for about a year with few arguments and no real blow ups to speak of. The honeymoon period was over and they were now in some amorphous new phase that felt like roots going down without them actually going down, like into a planting pot perhaps but not into the ground. Marriage was not out of the question, but Laura was gun shy having been through a few ugly break ups.

The idea of children roamed her imagination and circled her dreams, not so far fetched as it was a year ago or a year before that. At 31, she began to notice the baby strollers on the street. Some were getting to look like small cars, or playpens on wheels. You only go round once, she mused. She excelled at functional design and fixing things. You saw it in the feng shui interplay in their apartment of the low furniture, varied plantlife and varying light and shadow playing with each other like a silhouette puppet show moving around the room. She was the light and he the shadow, she the sun and he the moon. Her face gave off light and his absorbed and reflected it back. When they made love there was an astronomical eclipse.

Laura told her friends she was getting rid of birth control for a while and re-setting her internal clock to its natural sequence, to the call of the wild in her. She would howl like a wolf under the full moon in a mating call to Adam. He answered, sometimes, not as much as she would wish but he answered. Adam felt strongly for Laura, not the warm fuzzies but a solid, consistent and respectful commitment that had deepened in their year together. The warm fuzzies could come later, but for now Laura suited him.

Why didn't he come to bed with her? What was he doing in there so late? Adam frequently stayed up late in his work nook after Laura went to bed. That bothered her. It was the one thing that could ruin them. It grated on her and tested her patience. She wasn't exactly hurt but her pride stung and she caught her tongue a few times from blurting out an insult or accusation. There were tense moments some mornings, but he seemed so naive and innocent when she brought it up that later she felt guilty. Still, she couldn't help but imagine him flirting with women and who knows what else, what digital depravities he was capable of. She thought she knew him, but she thought she knew the other guys too. Her friends said to watch out for this guy. Laura listened and read stuff. She bought and wore sexy night wear and scented their bedroom with jasmine and Japanese incense. Still he hung back and bided his time into the wee hours, alone in his work nook. She heard him pacing or his desk chair creaking and occasionally the grinding of a pencil being sharpened.

Adam was actually collected and steady with a low key ego, the kind of partner frequently brought home to mama and with good results. He wasn't into the weird or deviant stuff she suspected. When he wasn't working, he read or watched TV, ran the treadmill or looked through coffee table art books. They had quite the collection of those. Adam brought a new one home at least once a month. That's all he brought home, other than his work and a few groceries. They piled up around the house, Cassatt, Munch, Klimt, African Art, Frida Kahlo, to name just a few. After hours, when Laura went to sleep, he perused them with a quiet ardor quite at odds with his understated personality. He felt like a child left alone in a candy shop or waking up on Christmas morning. The tension was exquisite. He would fall into bed, finally, at 2 or 3 am next to Laura, his head still warm and brimming with visions of variables in the texture composition and lighting of the art and not fall asleep until first light.

The cat took Laura's side. The little monster did her best growl whenever Adam glanced her way or got too close. Perhaps for the first time, he took a good hard look at the fur-ball one night. He forgot her name, which was Furdinand. It momentarily dazzled and mesmerized him, which startled the cat, which began to back away. As she retreated he saw and drew in his mind a profusion of mostly browns oranges and pinkish whites swirling in on around and through her half shell ears that tried to be pointy and which formed a kind of protective halo over pure turquoise eyes, a thin sophisticated white-stripe runway nose leading down to the vaguest hint of an orange tip above two black-leatherish openings for breathing and a mysterious whiskered mouth hidden like a cave, sans lips, behind blacks and whites. This painting and the one of Laura's pretzel pose with socked foot flickered through his head, pulsed down into his heart and sprang onto canvases in Adam's imagination. He wanted badly to paint and share them with her so she would quit worrying what he did on his computer after she went to bed. That thorny issue, that unpleasantry should also be put to bed, he thought.

Two ripe avocados sat and relaxed one evening in a yellow-brown wicker basket in the brightly lit white kitchen near the window next to the sink. It was a Thursday night. Laura wanted guacamole and a drink. Adam volunteered to make the guacamole. He had been mentally absent from the relationship lately. He knew that. She remarked on it. Furdinand had to weigh in on it of course so she growled. He took the hint, rolled up his sleeves and headed into the kitchen where the single high-watt lightbulb hanging above the thin plexiglass barrier seemed poised to give him the third degree about his mental and emotional whereabouts, as in: 'where were you on such and such a night when Laura went to sleep alone, again? ' As he entered, he froze. Shafts of yellow and pink light attacked the defenseless avocados through the kitchen window at about a twenty degree angle from the sinking setting sun off in the distance. The avocados appeared to dance and spin like whirling dervishes or dreidels. The colors wrapped around them as they spun. Adam couldn't peel and mush them at that moment any more than Count Leo could have killed off Anna halfway through the novel:

> "No Stiva", she said, "I'm lost, lost, worse than lost. I can't say yet that all is over. On the contrary, I feel that it's not over. I'm an overstrained string that must snap. But it's not ended yet … "

He grabbed a small piece of blank paper off of a pad that they used for grocery lists and began to mark it up with a pencil. The clock on the wall ticked. He sketched and erased sketched and erased over and over ten, fifteen, twenty strokes. He erased the heavy lines, blew away the erasures and then turned the pencil on its side for lighter lines. Or he erased the lighter lines and penciled in heavier. Or both on the same line. He worked fast and with a sense of urgency because that light would not hold and who knew when or if it would catch those angles and colors again. Shadows had already begun to gather around the bottom of the wicker basket and were moving up. Laura sat waiting in the next room, hungry and still a little chafed at his late night absences from their bed. He wasn't going to bury her suspicions standing around drawing. He could hear her phone impatiently clacking out texts and other messages one after another. His ears burned.

> *"And going over the events of the last few days it seemed to her that she saw a confirmation of this terrible idea. The fact that he had not dined at home yesterday and the fact that he insisted on their taking separate sets of rooms in Petersburg, and that even now he was not coming to her alone, as though he were trying to avoid meeting her face to face."*

Some friends joined them. They all sat down with the guac and drinks. More liquids were furnished. The guac ran out and pizza was ordered. Pretty soon everyone loosened up and glistened. Laura went and sat down close to Adam with her drink in a show of ownership. She kissed him on the mouth and he blushed. Signaled by the kiss, the cat jumped on his lap, landing on one of his testicles, pinching it and making him grimace slightly. The others laughed. Laura put her mouth close to Adam's ear and whispered she wasn't going to bed that night without him, come what may, emphasis on the word come. Alejandra, a friend, chimed in that they made a beautiful couple, if only Adam would smile a little more. At this, Adam colored and produced a kind of sweet, upturned expression about the mouth and gently tossed the cat on the floor where it meowed out a protest just as its paws touched.

Alejandra cut a striking figure, with fierce black eyes, thick dark eyebrows, a warm embracing smile and boasting broad shoulders and long strong legs from biking and hiking, often with Laura. The drinks helped Adam to frame her on his mental canvas floating through a window horizontally as in a Marc Chagall. Her wide expressive lips asked to be painted in generous tones, possibly with tiny pointed speckles of soft pinks, browns and misty greens. The rest of her rich complexion and noble profile appeared to him in various coffee-with-cream beiges and light browns, depending on the light, with a mysterious aura of the sea surrounding her. Or he would depict her as a Peruvian goddess mounted on a majestic amphibious horse as it rises out of the ocean onto the beach, rider and beast dripping and gleaming in the sun. She has on denim shorts, no shirt, cowboy boots that cover most of her solid calves and her resplendent black hair is pulled back into a long thick wrapped braid falling down over her left shoulder.

> *"He walked down, for a long while trying not to look long at her, as at the sun, but seeing her; as one does the sun, even without looking."*

EPILOGUE

Laura and Adam have two grown children. They never married. Laura was chicken. Adam didn't mind, he saw nothing compelling in marriage. They eat, drink, live and breathe art. After his first four critically acclaimed paintings, Laura jumped into the deep end where Adam caught her with open arms. The warm fuzzies followed… They were to remain lifelong partners and equals in everything.

> *"He felt now that he was not simply close to her, but that he did not know where he ended and she began."*

Laura manages all of the business aspects. She is the caretaker of the vibe that feeds Adam's muse. The children lead eclectic lives and careers outside the conventional paths of schooling, college, a job in marketing, tech development or whatever. They live creatively in different time zones, different from their parents and from each other.

Adam's work hangs in the local art museum on loan from New York. The children are in town for the retrospective, and they all go together to see it on a Sunday. In a corner of the first room hangs Laura, well not exactly Laura, but her irrepressible socked foot and the rest of her up to her waist. It is painted in dark tones silhouettes and shadows. Further on, in the next room, a brash Furdinand snarls and bursts forth, looking quite alive and vibrant even though she died ten years ago. The magically lit avocados dominate the final room. Adam painted them off of the small grocery list paper onto a big canvas where they will now dance and spin forever in museums everywhere. People wander from room to room stopping in front of these and many other skilled works. They bring their hands up around their chins and whisper wise observations to their friends and partners. Some wear headphones through which Laura provides expert narration with nuanced commentary. The patrons don't know that the artist, Laura and their children are 'in the house.'

Among the other exhibited works are a deft intimate portrait of Laura, "Alejandra In Boots"—which has sold dozens of signed lithographs to collectors— and a self-portrait. Adam paintedhimself standing in front of an easel painting, his sleeves rolled up and a coffee table full of art books behind him. Beyond the coffee table, Furdinand is fussing with a ball of yarn and to the left of that, Laura's tiny socked foot pokes out from between her twisted thighs. The kitchen in their old apartment is in the back of the self-portrait, bathed in bright whites except for two greenish-brown avocados at the rear drenched in sun and waiting to be sketched and then mushed up and eaten.

"All the variety, all the charm, all the beauty of life is made up of light and shadow.
Levin sighed and made no reply."

The quotes in this story are from translations of *Anna Karenina* by Leo Tolstoy that are in the public domain.

LESSONS FROM THE KITCHEN

JO CURTAIN

We are light and shadow. At a cellular level, mind-bending, skin-tingling sensations – the duality between who we are and who we don't want to be. The trick is to find balance. – Narrator.

I see Vivi decompose before me. Precarious and pale, she is languid stillness. A claustrophobic shadow creeps in from the corners. I feel the swampy folds of air wrap around me. I feel the discomfort swell in my guts. It is mine to own, but I push it away. She blinks hard and turns towards me. I am uncertain whether she recognises me.

Sound, but her lips barely move. *The cancer is sucking the life out of me.*

I lift the lid of the bowl of vegetable broth. *It's Nonnina's recipe.*

Some spark returns. *Acquacotta?*

Yes! I say a little too enthusiastic.

She says *I will vomit.* I want to tell her she needs this, but I don't. Instead, I lift the spoon to her lips and say, *sip it. Just sip.*

The edges of the room begin to shift. Vivi is dissolving. The ground is diminished from absorbing the years I spent remembering her as everything—sturdy, invincible, and ageless. I never allowed for all the nuances of light and shadow, what we ignore, and what we deny—neglecting truths and the opportunity to grow.

Eyes.

Closed.

When I leave the hospital, it is early evening. The bus's headlights seem to be the only corporal form in the veil-like light. Quite shimmering. I feel for my cheek. I feel for my existence and slowly fall behind the long line of people. One by one. Crammed in with people looking at their phones. Listening to music. Reading. Jarring with each stop. Again and again. Outside, the skyscrapers fade into half-darkness. The city keeps moving. It hit me. People don't stop. It is the ambiguity of life—an orchestrated tension like that of light and shadow—within and surrounding. Tears edge my eyes, and I get off the bus in an embarrassed flush—a gigantic despair hisses into the darkness. But then the feeling recedes as quickly as it formed—

I

know

where

I

am.

Pulsating, limitless light. Ordered. I have spent most of my life in the kitchen. The big and brash, industrial crisp white flashes in the chaos. Multiple pots and pans boiling, simmering and frying and an abundance of carefully placed tea towels. Strong hands and smeared aprons. No matter where, through the windows and doors of people's homes are messy corners of sprawling jars of spices. Shopping lists pinned to humming fridges. Breadcrumbs and shrivelled onion skins on wood cutting boards. An abrupt whoosh of heat and Pop! Eclectic collections. Memories and tangible items. Capturing the movement of time and place. I hadn't yet learnt that everything plays out in the kitchen.

... shadow itself is of the light – Frank Lloyd Wright
Before everything, there was only light. My earliest memories were in the kitchen watching my mother prepare the ricotta-filled puff pastry shells – sfogliatelle. Comfort clings. Ting! White tiles and stainless steel breathe like dreamy harmony. Blinding light and toddler's fingers smash ricotta into the highchair tray. Shadows came later in the form of forearms and hands reaching out, brushing away tears, disturbing memories, and disrupting views. Darkening my world. The inevitability of people breaking down. I hadn't yet learnt how to measure anguish or   how

years

run

away

stealing things. Stealing the people that I love. It took me a long time to accept that everything, no matter how beautiful and loved or how resilient and robust, will eventually break.

Enrico's cheery voice—Vivi's sometime lover, brings me back to the street. I wipe away the tears, smooth my shirt and wander over to him.

I'm on break. Come, sit with me, cara.

Hey Rico, I sit on the milk crate beside him.

He knows to ignore the flushed appearance. I am starving. His restaurant is famous for its spaghetti alla puttanesca sauce. Enrico calls to the chef to cook a bowl for me. Sitting next to him, I feel the shades of shadow penetrate, taking me somewhere else, different from where Enrico is or where I'd ever been. I am at the bottom of a canyon where no one can reach me. Enrico takes hold of my hand and abruptly pulls me out. My food is ready. I perk up; it's incredible! Chef smiles jubilantly. Then I remembered the first meal Vivi cooked for me was fish puttanesca.

Between now and the beginning, I have had my own troubles. Torments of loss and fear. I was ten years old when my parents died in a car accident. Alone. Until Vivi gathered me up.

Everything will be okay. She dried my tears.

All I could do was gesture a response: my Mamma's sister, my Zietta, my Vivi. I arrived at her apartment, a refurbished warehouse on a historical wharf that once breathed working-class Sydney. An open-plan, high-ceiling light crisscrossed the room. The deep balcony gave the illusion that the apartment was floating on the harbour. The kitchen beckoned me in.

She told me to sit on the stool. I am going to cook your favourite food. My eyes said *how do you know?*

Ah, once you taste this, it will be your favourite.

This was how Vivi looked after you.

She stood slicing onion and tomatoes. No garlic; she was seeking sweetness. *Now. For Nonnina's contribution,* Vivi winked and placed the cast iron pan onto the stovetop. Undefeated. The tomatoes simmered, breaking down. Little fish sautéed in a skillet. Grilled zucchini. Then, she brought them together, creating a beautiful symbiosis. It was like time had turned back. Confident and light. Albeit briefly, joy returned to my heart.

All the variety, all the charm, all the beauty of life is made up of light and shadow. – Leo Tolstoy.

Slow rising. Cut, twisted, pitted, and quartered, the plums break down slowly. My desire for balance keeps me alert. In another pot, the sound of water boiling fills the room, and I gently work the jars into the water. The lights on the window fill with thoughts about Vivi. My heart dims with a strange guilt. What had I done? Nothing. I had done nothing. An inner turmoil was trying to make sense of a new reality and understand Vivi now. The far corners of the kitchen darken. I know it is convenient to say that I am now an adult, but I have learnt that what I once relied on to get me through has fallen apart.

I count the years

sixteen when I began cooking under the guidance of Vivi. I poured everything into it. I worked part-time at Victoria Street Deli and spent all the money I earned on cookbooks and practising, perfecting recipes cooking for Vivi, her stream of lovers and friends. And the simmering frustration boiling over because sometimes everything was not enough.

I smile to remember. The seeds Vivi planted, knowing that one day it would open my eyes like every time I made a mistake, she'd say

Most recipes are malleable and adaptable to change.
You can take from here and from there and add what you need.

The duality of what I need and what I want, what I acknowledge and what I ignore and what I can control and what I can't. When I was little, I imagined two worlds existed. This world and a hidden world. Because I didn't know how to feel. I didn't know what to feel. I didn't know how to feel until

shafts of light
flicker across the
surface of the
workbench,
sliding
beneath the rounded
corners
laughing,
crafting
patterns on the wall
revealing
Here is this world.

I am a woman of nearly 32, nearly the age Vivi was when she became my guardian. I am learning how to cry to release everything like I've never done before. I no longer live with Vivi but have not drifted far from the floating apartment. I cook Vivi's favourite dish, minestrone with prawns. I count the steps because a minestrone doesn't forgive. You can bend it but don't neglect it. Like any good drama, I know the traditionalists will scream scandal, but I think back to what Vivi said a bit from here, a bit from there and what you need. I am learning. I am learning how everyone breaks. Her cancer has spread to her liver.

Sun and clouds.

Balance.

I prepare two bowls to take to the hospital.

MARSHMALLOWS

OSHADHA PERERA

When I was four, I used to sit on a bean bag in the corner of your office, watching the 28″ TV screen. You had a whole stack of nature documentaries piled beside the TV. The hum of your fingers tapping the keyboard was background noise against David Attenborough's voice, as I watched red crabs on Christmas Island cover the roads in a crimson blanket.

Sometimes, you would stay in the office after work and make us hot chocolate. One marshmallow for you, three for me. We would watch blue macaws flying in the Amazon and ants walking in a single file, carrying leaves for their nests. The camera would pan over glaciers in Antarctica, and you would comment on how cute the little Emperor penguins looked as they paddled from side to side, tiny wings spread apart. As soon as the seals started appearing, though, you'd fake a yawn and switch to Tom and Jerry. We'd always be back in your car by six, and I would draw pictures on the fogged windows while you drove us home.

I can still remember my first day of school, when you stood beside the gate, waving at me. It was a frosty morning and you had forgotten your jacket, but you were still there when I looked through the classroom window fifteen minutes later. Eventually, it started to rain, and the window became too blurry for me to see you. Later that day, I asked you not to cut fruit into triangles and circles like you used to do when packing my lunch. You said no worries, you'd do that. I never saw the smile fade away from your face.

You still drove me to your office after school on Fridays. I would watch nature documentaries like I used to do, while you typed strings of numbers into Excel. After a while, you'd make us hot chocolate and collapse onto the bean bag beside me. I would smile and drink it, pretending to ignore that you forgot the marshmallows. The close-up of swimming sardines would change to a wide shot of tuna and a couple of hammerhead sharks. When you lifted the remote to switch to Tom & Jerry, I would tell you that I can watch the water turn red and carcasses sink down; that I'm not a little kid anymore.

I got my first job when I turned sixteen. It was the afternoon shift at High Street Café & Restaurant, one block away from your office. By seven, the café would be crowded. Families would fill the four-seat tables in the corner, and point to the eggplant parmigiana with roast lamb, and a kid-sized meal with hot chocolate. The chef made the most wonderful parmigiana I know of, and I didn't get in his way, because the last time I cooked eggplants, they tasted like burnt rubber and smoke. Hot chocolate, though, would always be my job. The milk went in first, and then two spoons of chocolate powder. I would mix with the spoon at an angle, the way you used to do, so that the froth would touch the brim of the cup but wouldn't overflow.

On some days, you would slide into the parking slot in front of the café and wait for me. I guess you didn't want to go home to an empty house, to switch on the lights and hear the silence echo off the humid air. On other nights, though, you'd still be working when my shift ended. I would walk from the café to your office, watching your windows glow against the sleeping buildings. I would wait in the car for you to finish work, thinking about the stacks of nature DVDs sitting on your table. The ride home would be silent.

I used to count police cars and fire trucks whenever I saw them passing. If there was only one police car, I'd imagine a speeding driver on the run. If there were two, I'd think of someone calling 111 while hiding from a burglar. That day, two ambulances and two fire trucks passed the café. Minutes later, a firefighter in a high-vis vest asked us to evacuate the building. Outside, the air smelt slightly burnt. The next block was flaming in bright orange, melting debris occasionally falling onto the road.

You had been in your office when the fire had struck. I ran around the fire trucks, ducking under water hoses, trying to find you. One of the windows in your office was broken, smoke spilling out of it. Bright flames dancing in the dark room. My lungs were burning, each breath becoming more and more of a struggle. I still hadn't found you when I felt my phone vibrating in my pocket.

The nurse said it wasn't serious, that you would be discharged in about a week. Your voice would return to normal, and the clawing feeling in your chest would disappear soon enough. The burn mark on your left cheek would stay there, though. You could watch it in the mirror every day and tell adventure stories about it. It would be a story I would carry with me, a reminder that I was one block away when it happened; that if I had been more alert and seen the smoke rising, I could've helped you before the firefighters arrived.

That night, we watched Nature. Zebra foals were playing in the grasslands, running through the tall blades of grass. I took a week's leave from the café to spend the evenings with you. This time, though, I didn't switch the TV off, because I knew that the lion wouldn't be able to touch the zebras when they stampeded through the savannah; that sardines wouldn't get eaten when they swam in a tight group, rotating and changing direction, camouflaged against the light filtering into the sea. I made hot chocolate for you, bubbles dangling on the edge of the cup, but not falling over.

Three marshmallows for me, one for you.

IN THE LINE OF DUTY

JAKE RICHARDS

Tremsdale is traditionally known as 'the busy station' where they say 30 years ago, you'd have a structure fire every week easy—a place where you don't sleep and don't expect to. I'm not sure if the old fellas are just exaggerating or if it really was that busy but it's different now. I've been in the job for three years and I could sure do with a few good burns.

Everyone still talks about working out of Trema like it's the front line—'Oooh you're out at Station 2 for the next few months, don't bother packing dinner.' In summer it can be busy it's true. With kids lighting up the bush outside of town and dickheads burning out cars, being nuisances on the train line and the occasional 2-bedroom cinder block housing commission burn. But mostly, time out at Trema is cruisy and slow. Shifts take a l-l-o-o-n-n-g-g time to pass. It's a good time to pick a good TV series to watch with the guys or get in the habit of going to the gym. It's the sort of place where you wake up after getting six hours sleep on your second night shift and stare at yourself in the mirror feeling a combination of being stoked that you got paid to sleep and also feeling a bit guilty about getting paid taxpayer dollars and wondering how you could better contribute to society.

I was out at Tremsdale Station with some really great blokes for six weeks. I liked everyone on shift, but I especially liked Eddie. Eddie is the sort of guy that makes you laugh no matter what you're doing or how mundane or dark the situation is. He is quick, but he is also very smart and, most importantly, he's kind. We got a rare one on him one night as he fell asleep in an armchair. We drew all over his face, rolled up a piece of paper and stuck it in his mouth like a cigarette. He slept like a baby through the whole thing. That's Eddie for you, he's sleeping, and he still makes you laugh...

That night the bells went off at 2:00am. The burning bright lights beat down on my face as I lay there under the bed sheet. I quickly wiped my eyes before staring at the pager to read the job message. It took a while to focus on the screen—it was an alarm call to a local supermarket complex.

Nothing big. If the pager read 'STRUCTURE FIRE' or 'ROAD CRASH RESCUE' we'd have been falling over each other rushing to the turnout. But as it was, we all sauntered with only slight haste to get the gear on and climb in the truck within the acceptable 2 minutes. I noticed a tear in my turnout overpaints. I really should get those repaired.

Tim was driving and he hit the 'open' button for the engine bay doors. The rattle of the doors opening was drowned out as Tim started the truck and pulled out onto the road. No one talked as we drove the short way to the complex. It was often like this on a call out—a space between preparation and operation. We glided through the seemingly empty suburb. Eddie and I were going through our routine. We switched the handheld radios to the allocated channel, I turned the thermal camera on, and he grabbed the gas detector. We sat there holding our helmets as we looked out the window and watched the flashing blue and red lights momentarily paint the houses as we drove past.

We arrived on scene feeling complacent. Tim pulled the truck up outside and there was barely anyone else in the car park. We put our helmets on and walked up to the familiar main doors to the building; we opened it and approached the alarm panel in the foyer of the supermarket complex. We must have been to this place a few dozen times for different alarm calls, and it was never anything exciting... but this time there was a smell. It smelled like a mix of burning plastic and something a bit more organic. Eddie and I looked at each other; I saw his eyes flick upwards towards the ceiling, and I noticed a wispy white smoke haze floating up near the roof that was getting thicker and moving in a playful way. 'Shit, there's a fire!' I heard the officer call. The smoke was coming from a small bakery premise that was separated from the main area by a pull-out wire concertina style wall you often see in big shopping complexes. The officer started talking into his fist microphone and the radio chatter faded into the background as I scrambled to get my breathing apparatus on. While Timmy went back to the truck to roll out a 38mm hose from the pump, I found a hose reel attached to the wall of the supermarket complex, dragged it out and placed it on the ground next to the pull-out wire wall. I couldn't use the hose until we dealt with that wire wall.

It took me a while to fumble around and get my flash hood out of my pocket and get my BA and gloves on as I was still in a fluster over the unexpected development from an alarm call at sleepy Trema Station. I wasn't disappointed—I love a fire—but was just caught out of rhythm.

We were 'on air'. We had about 30 minutes of working time before we had to come out—35 if we conserved air.

Eddie and I had trouble opening the wire concertina wall dividing the bakery from the rest of the multi tenancy shopping centre.
I lifted up the pins of the gate with a hooligan tool while Eddie hit it with a sledgehammer—reefing it unlocked. We were able to push the wall aside. I turned my helmet light on as well as the plastic streamlight torch hanging from my turnout coat and we advanced into the wafty pea soup coloured smoke.

It didn't feel like a serious fire as it wasn't hot, and the smoke was grey white and not pulsating or moving quickly. It seemed like something was smouldering rather than burning.

Visibility was super poor. I was the first inside the building—holding the nozzle. Eddie was number two, pulling the hose. We followed the right-hand wall, searching for the fire. As it was late and the bakery had long since been locked up for the night, we were pretty confident there was no one in there.

But then I saw a faint light through the smoke in front of me. It couldn't be... As I moved through the soupy fog, I noticed the light again, and I was shocked, confused and quite concerned. I noticed that the light I was watching was moving... As I moved towards it, the intensity of the light's movement increased. It was hard to keep track of it through the thick, creamy smoke.

I was wondering how there could be someone in there. Maybe it was a baker who came in early to start on the pastries and bread? They work early, right? Maybe they caused a fire and became disoriented in the smoke and couldn't find their way out. It's happened to the best of us. I've been caught out in a building before when I have let go of the hose and ended up at the opposite side of the room. It was scary... Maybe the baker had a medical episode like a heart attack and had passed out and caused the pies to burn? And then woke up in a bakery full of smoke? Either way this must be a toxic atmosphere—dangerous to breathe and potentially deadly—despite the apparent absence of a major developing fire.

I moved quicker towards the light which seemed to be franticly trying to get somewhere... to get out of the smoke or towards me. I urgently focussed on reaching whoever this person was to pull them out of there. Those stupid wire walls would be impossible to get past if you couldn't see. They couldn't survive long in this... I felt Eddie following me and I cast aside some chairs and a bakery table between me and the casualty. I tried to tell Eddie what I was doing but surprise, surprise the radio was playing up. I couldn't talk to him, but I knew he was there. He was always there. I was careful to keep a foot on the right-hand wall as I crouched and crawled along the ground, so I didn't get disoriented. My plan was to reach the casualty and follow the hose back out as the quickest way to bring them to safety. I'd then return to find the fire and properly search the building for other people.

The light moved quicker; I moved quicker. Sweat was beading down my mask and it was starting to fog up. I could see a red glow flickering, pulsating in the distance on my left. I felt a slight warmth through my jacket and overpants on that side. That must be the fire. I'd deal with that later. The casualty was more important as they needed me NOW. The light was getting closer, and I felt I could almost reach out to it. I was calling out almost running on my haunches then…

Bang! I hit something! It knocked me down and it took me a while to right myself to feel a smooth hard surface in front of me and then bang! Bang! Eddie hit me from behind and we both hit the surface together.

It was a moment of stunned silence as we lay there in a tangled mess. Eddie was the first to cry out with laughter as we rolled around in the smoke-filled wet room in front of what we realised was a large glass mirror. We untangled ourselves from the hose and managed to get on our knees again. I had tears of laughter in my eyes as I realised the absurdity of thinking the reflection of my own torch and helmet light was someone that needed rescuing! Eddie gave me a playful push as he waved his torch in front of the mirror and watched the reflection mimic him.

Anticlimactically we located a pile of smouldering paper cups on top of a refrigerator. We wet the cups down, inspected the roof space for further fire extension and ventilated the building. As Eddie and I walked out of the bakery back to the 'fresh air base' to get changed we sheepishly agreed we would keep this little incident between us for the time being.

Later on, in the truck on the drive back to station, Timmy said, 'I thought you two must have gotten lost in an oven; it seemed like a long time before you knocked down the fire.'

Eddie gave me a wink and said, 'On reflection, it did take us a while.'

SUN CAT WITH SMOKE FOR A BODY

BRENDAN CALDWELL

Faith, the youngest, begins to draw many pictures. Her mother wishes the pictures would be of anything else, but no, they are of cats. Faith pencils them and crayons them in the waning summer heat as her brothers run in and out of the house, squawking and pulling t-shirts until the cloth rips. Her mother scolds the boys and they fall away. She feels a keen remorse—the immediate desire to call them back and throw the torn fabric in the bin with happy nonchalance. It doesn't matter, their mother would say, though her eyes would not show this feeling to be true. In any case, the boys are gone again, and only Faith remains with her mother now, dragging greasy purple lines across toothy paper to make yet another immense and bulbous cat.

What is this one, her mother asks.

Plum cat who steals plums, says Faith. She puts the page aside and at once takes up another, to scratch, to draw again. Her mother walks away and will not look.

In the cooling nights Faith's mother lies in bed and counts the weekends left before school begins again, time when her hands may be free of clutching shoes and saying 'no' to every loud demand. She feels clean sheets in the dark, fresh today. Sleep drags at her as flat, slow waves. Then, the sensation of something sharp and small. She finds in the gloom, with sleepful hands, a loose lost claw in bed, shed from their cat, Hatchet, which she pinches now between finger and thumb like a plectrum. She strums the sharp point along her own calf, her knee, her thigh, feeling in the fur-black darkness of night, sensation without language. The scrape of a little fossil, no more. Somewhere else in the house, with fresh claws, Hatchet purrs.

She resolves to sleep and not to dream tonight of Faith's father, reaching upward. Of that snap of tree and human.

Summer ends in fits of rain and tears. The boys don their uniforms with the sluggish body memory of scratchy acrylic days spent frowning over arithmetic books. They know what comes of this and they cling to her in wretched clumps all the way to the school gate. One by one, they start to cry; the fearlessness of sun is gone.

I want dad, one of them says. And all the rest say nothing. Only Faith, who stood ready to leave the house that morning with an impatient face, walks past the gate without stopping. Her waterproof shoes depict whiskers and smiles. Her little mouth rests without expression now, her goal within impassive reach. Eventually, the boys follow. One of them must be torn away by teacher's hands. The teacher meets his mother's eyes, delivering a full and funereal pity. She has come out to help, thinks Faith's mother, because she has learned what happened. It is kind of her, and yet the pity stings.

By the end of the first week of school, Faith's mother is called in at pick-up. Faith's teacher and another teacher offer tea and solemn smiles, even as they show the countless images that Faith has drawn. The colours are deep and vibrant and seem to make a sound with the force of their clashing. Music cat with money. Cat holding a rake. Umbrella cat with juice for rain. Many of the cats are recurring images from her summer drawing. Faith's mother greets them with nods of recognition, strangely grateful that there is at least someone else in the room with whom she is already closely familiar.

The teachers use the words 'coping mechanism' as if Faith's mother has not heard this phrase before. She nods and says, 'oh yes?' allowing them to believe this is the case. They agree to do nothing for now, but wait some more. Perhaps Faith, they reason, will draw herself out. But they also agree to watch. She leaves, squeezing her daughter's hand, perhaps humiliated, perhaps grateful.

At home, Faith piles the stack of papers, curling at their corners, next to Hatchet's sleeping spot on the arm of the sofa. Hatchet yawns and chews the corners of the illustrations, loudly smacking some part of his barbed tongue as he nibbles at the paper. An experiment in pre-digestion. Faith's mother watches their cat chew and feels her hands curl and tense into talons, a spike of disgust and hate.

He loved this cat.

She leaves the room before it overwhelms her and Hatchet only looks on as she leaves, uncaring eyes noting her speed and nothing else. In Hatchet's mute gaze she continues to find alternating feelings day by day. As he scratches the carpet, fear. As he shits into his litter box, shame. As he sleeps peacefully, rage. When he climbs above her children on the furniture or stretches out on the top step of the stairs, she leaves the room, heart pounding.

The day she finally hires the tree surgeon, Hatchet is locked inside with her. He paces and screeches through the window, watching as a chainsaw is put to the only tree in the garden. She watches too and worries what the two men outside think of her, cutting down a perfectly healthy ash. Probably they have to do this all the time, she thinks.

They ask if she wants to keep the cuttings for firewood, and she shakes her head. The men pause for the merest second, perhaps expecting some explanation, that she has no fireplace, that it isn't needed, until one of them curls his chin into a shrugging frown and hands her a receipt for the job.

When the children come home with her later and see what's happened, they look out, chewing toast. "The tree," says one of the boys, simply, matter-of-factly, as if finally getting the answer to a crossword puzzle. They walk away. Only Faith stays to watch as Hatchet, free to roam once again, clambers onto the bright, exposed trunk, which will be left to harden in the winter. A pockmark on the grass, immovable, forever.

As the days pass from light to dark, Faith continues to draw her cats, whispering to herself now. Her mother asks, already knowing the answer, if her daughter would like to draw something else. She leads by example, draws a beach, a boat, a tractor, a pig. Faith continues to draw a vast yellow cat. Trails of scarlet rise from the animals back. Darkest grey is clawed onto the page in chaotic patches. Around the cat's feet lie piles and piles of what might be pages. Or leaves.

Faith's mother asks: what is this one called?

Faith says: Sun cat with smoke for a body.

Faith's mother gives in.

She picks up an orange crayon and takes a blank page from her daughter's pile. Faith's mother draws the only cat she sees every day, Hatchet. She draws him sitting high in a tree, too high. She draws her husband beneath, looking up. She draws the hot sun, the barbecue, smoking with promise. She does not draw the ladder, nor the broken branch, nor the broken spine, nor her husband's crumpled body, his bark-stained jacket. And yet, when she is finishing with her picture, she sees it all there, behind, like the dappled light that burns behind the leaves of a tree in summer. She draws these specks of light. She does not draw Faith, standing with her father.

On the sofa nearby, Hatchet sits up, yawns, and lies back down. Faith's mother rises, leaves her daughter to finish drawing Sun Cat, and takes her own page to the stack close to where Hatchet lies.

She looks at the cat her husband loved as she places down the page. He looks back with half-closed lids, chin on his paws, comfortable but vaguely alert. Finally, he closes his eyes, taking this offering peaceably. Later he will rise, stretch, chew the corner of this page, and leave to patrol elsewhere.

For now, Faith's mother walks back and sits with her daughter again, who takes her mother's hand without looking up. With her other hand, Faith continues to draw Sun Cat, smoke rising from its body.

MILK TEETH

BELLA RONA

Liza is careful not to break it—the milk skin draped over the teaspoon handle like a sheet pulled taut on a line, swaying slightly. She thinks of summer: air heady with pollen, forest hysterical with flowers, panes of yellow sunlight in the kitchen. She stirs a heaped spoon of hot chocolate into the milk and sets it down in front of Maisie.

'I got them all right,' Maisie says.

'Did Mrs T give you the answers?'

'I just know them.'

Liza runs her eyes down the page. 'You've left three of them blank.'

'What can I have if I finish it?'

Liza laughs and swipes the mug off the table. 'This is mine for now,' she says, but Maisie's stomach rumbles and she sets it back down and kisses her temple twice.

'Can we go to the cinema?'

Liza pulls out a chair and finds Spud beneath the table, drooling in her sleep, and Maisie's feet tucked under her belly. She pulls up the Odeon website on her phone, finds something Pixar is playing in an hour. It's over £15 for two tickets. They'd need to stop for fuel on the way.

'Cinema's closed today, babe,' she says. 'Let's go for a walk.'

Maisie pushes her chair back and, standing, writes *10/10* at the top of her worksheet. She runs to get her coat.

'Come on, Spuddle,' she shouts from the hallway, and the dog wakes, rolls onto her feet and careers out of the room.

In the morning, Liza watches Maisie skilfully decapitate her boiled egg and march a strip of toast towards it.

'Mayday! Mayday!' she says, and plunges the toast into the egg's molten core. She pulls it out, dripping, and crams the whole thing into her mouth. Liza nuzzles the iron into the pleats of the skirt. When she looks up, Maisie is holding a strip of toast over Spud's open jaws.

'Nope,' says Liza. The toast wriggles.

'I said no.'

Maisie drops the toast and Spud chews, confused and delighted.

'Why d'you do that?'

'She wanted it.'

Liza spots the worksheet on the table, its cheetah print of greasy marks. She walks over and scans it.

'Wrong.' She points at the first answer.

'I haven't checked it yet.'

Her finger tracks down the page. 'Wrong. Blank. Wrong.'

'I'll do it now.'

'What's Mrs T going to think?' She hears the ferocity in her voice and inhales, softening, but already there are tears in Maisie's eyes. Maisie pads across the kitchen in her woolly tights and disappears into the living room. Liza follows and finds her lying on the floor, tangled in the dog, running her hand down her camel-coloured flank.

'She can come with us to school if you want,' Liza says.

They cut through the park. Maisie is telling a story about a boy who ran and skated on his lunch tray from one end of the canteen to the other when Spud sees a squirrel and launches herself towards it. Maisie stumbles after her, screaming and laughing. Spud stops at the base of a tree—the squirrel gushes up the trunk —and barks.

'Come on, you daft thing,' Liza says. Maisie hands over the leash so she can cartwheel to the end of the path.

'What kinda dog is that?'

Liza turns to see an old man on a bench. He is wearing a long puffer jacket zipped up to his neck.

'Sorry?' she says.

'Dogs like that,' he says, pointing to Spud, who is watching Maisie cartwheel and jumping her front paws up as if to copy her, 'shouldn't be allowed near children.'

Liza squints at him and carries on across the park. Maisie wobbles in exaggerated wooziness, folding onto the grass, green stains on her freshly pressed skirt.

Even with the door slammed shut behind her, Liza's breath springs white in the hallway. She showers, allowing herself hot water for the length of a short, tinny song she plays from her phone, and puts on leggings beneath jeans. There are three new rejections in her email inbox. She tries calling the job centre but is put on hold and gives up after half an hour. She sits in the living room and eats a small, chalky apple.

Spud tries to jump up beside her on the sofa and lands on her stomach, sloping back onto the floor. She mewls and Liza lifts her onto her lap. Panting, Spud smiles the way Maisie smiles when she does her going-down-the-escalator mime. Along her snout is a white mark that stretches into the space between her eyes like a sail. Her nose and mouth are a pale mulberry, nearly identical to the shade of her collar. Outside, a woman restores a watermelon the size of a bowling ball to a torn paper bag. Liza's phone pings: *Hello I saw your leaflet...* She sits up and unlocks her phone.

'Spuddy,' she says. 'Someone has asked me to do two hours today.'

The house is a ten-minute walk along the canal and her throat is parched sore by the wind. The woman is called Kathleen and she wants to set up her new laptop and transfer some data from her old one. As Liza works, Kathleen keeps thanking her and bringing her cups of tea, NICE biscuits trembling on the saucer. Liza shows her how to set up a videocall so she can see her grandchildren when she speaks to them.

'You have kids, love?' she says.

'Two little ones,' Liza says without thinking.

'Lovely things, are they?'

'They are. Up to all sorts of mischief.'

'I bet.'

Liza doesn't turn away from the screen. 'One of them's a bit ill at the moment, actually.'

'They bring back more illnesses than they can count to when they're young.'

Liza takes a noisy sip of tea and imagines Spud disappearing into the splutter of kids at the school gate.

Kathleen gets Liza to set up a new email account and online grocery order and pays her the whole £40, even though the work has taken half the time she anticipated. She looks upset when Liza puts her coat on.

'Would these be of any use to you, love?' she says, and holds up a box depicting salt and pepper shakers that resemble hugging panda bears. 'I've never used them.'

Liza takes the box and touches Kathleen's arm.

'Thank you,' she says. Kathleen briefly rests her hand on Liza's.

The house is too quiet. She puts on her jogging playlist and goes up and down the stairs a few times, but she hasn't got much energy, and the music keeps cutting out with the internet. She unwraps the ceramic bears and takes them up to Maisie's room. She puts them on top of the bookcase. She can hear breathing—laboured, wet—and pulls back the quilt from the side of the bed. Spud is on her side, eyes half closed, between all the soft toys.

'What are you doing under there?' She crawls under the bed and strokes Spud's ear. Spud moves her head up for a chin scratch. Liza pulls out her phone. She opens her voicemail and plays the message, mouthing along to the words.

'Hi Liza, apologies for missing your call. I wanted to inform you that, given the results of the bloods, we'd like to do some more tests on Spud. Please give me a ring so we can arrange her next appointment.'

She keys in the number and balances the phone on her ear.

'Hello, Kelly from Pet World speaking.'

'Hello.'

'Hi.'

'Hi, it's Liza, Spud's owner.'

'Oh, hello Liza, hi.'

'Hi Kelly. I'm calling about test results.'

'Yes, so…'

'It's bad news.'

'There are some indicators that the growth could be malignant.' Kelly's voice is suddenly the voice of a politician.

'Right,' says Liza.

'We'd like to book Spud in for an ultrasound and go from there.'

Liza pulls Aladdin's arm out from where it is jammed under Spud's neck. 'How much will that cost?'

'Around seventy,' she says, clacking on her keyboard. 'When can you bring her in?'

'And if she has cancer–'

'We won't know until–'

'How much can I expect to spend over the course of her treatment?'

'It's very case dependent.'

'Ballpark.'

Spud growls quietly as she falls asleep.

'I'd say anywhere between two to ten thousand. But your insur–'

'It'd be cheaper to clone her.' Liza muzzles into Spud's chest.

'You can't put a price on love.'

Maisie emerges from the classroom clinging to Avery, who is slim and blonde and already looks like a teenager. They scan the crowd of parents until Avery spots her mother, who is also tall, slim and blonde. Liza watches the three of them push towards her.

'Mummy,' says Maisie, wrapping herself around Liza's leg.

'Hi beautiful.' She kisses her daughter's head.

'I don't think we've met yet,' says Avery's mother and Liza, suddenly aware of her sweatshirt, the fray of her hair across her shoulders, scoops up the woman's hand and shakes it.

'Our girls get along so well,' Liza says.

As if to demonstrate Maisie and Avery start to chase each other, figure-of-eighting around their mothers.

'They've just begged me for a playdate,' says the woman.

'We can definitely arrange–'

'Apparently there's some game they need to finish tonight.'

Maisie stops running and locks her arms around Liza's waist. 'Please? We're in the middle of Jungle Jungle.'

'Can we do yours?' the woman says. 'I've just painted Avery's room.'

The girls cheer and run off.

Liza precedes the others into the house and, as they hang up their coats and bags in the hallway, sprints around the kitchen, swiping crumbs off the surfaces and gathering stray dishes into the sink. She hears the girls scamper upstairs. The woman—Amber? Amy?—slinks into the room.

'Your daughter's smart, isn't she,' she says. 'Avery tells me they're the same colour on the reading scale.'

'Mm.' Liza fills the kettle. 'Maisie's always loved books. Sleeps with them under her pillow.'

'Cute.'

'She barely fits in the bed, what with the books and the dog.' Liza fishes a teabag out of the box.

A flash of something on the woman's face. 'The dog sleeps in the bed with her?'

Liza splits the teabag in her fist. She sweeps the granules into the sink and finds another.

'Milk and sugar?' she says, and the woman nods.

After an hour stringing together a conversation about the schools in the area, which parents are going to chaperone the upcoming trip to Fishbourne, what is going to be sold at Friday's bake sale, and finally how cold it is for this time of year, the girls appear, complaining that they're hungry.

Liza hugs her daughter to her. 'Avery and her mum probably have to–'

'Oh, we've got nowhere to be.'

Liza opens the fridge. There's a small pizza, enough for the girls to share.

'Let me,' says the woman, appearing behind her.

'God no, I'll—'

'No, seriously, you've let me invite myself into your home and waffle on about shortbread recipes, the least I could do is make dinner.'

'Of course not,' starts Liza, but the woman ushers her back to her seat. She watches the woman stand in front of her fridge as if she owns it—hand on the handle, shoulders square. She watches the woman take out the cream, the cheese, the eggs, the pasta, the butter, the bacon, the tomatoes, the salad leaves, the bread —and clank around with pans and pots until, spread out before her on the table, is all the food that is supposed to last them until the end of the week. The woman calls the girls down. Maisie, wide-eyed, opens her mouth but Liza gives her a look and she closes it again.

'Ew, why's there a raw egg on mine?' Avery says.

'That's how they do it in France,' her mother says.

Avery pushes her plate away. Maisie looks down at hers and copies her mother, stirring the yolk into the pasta. She sucks up a strand of tagliatelle, cream flicking onto her cheeks. She grins, takes a bigger mouthful. She pulls her friend's bowl back in front of her.

'It's really good,' she says. 'Try it.'

'Sorry.' Liza pushes her chair back. It grunts against the floorboards. 'I just need to go and check on the dog.' She picks up Spud's bowl and carries it to the living room. Spud is curled on the sofa. Liza pincers a jellied cube and holds it up to her. Spud sniffs.

'Good girl,' says Liza, as Spud latches her teeth around it. In the kitchen, she can hear Maisie explaining to Avery's mum the rules of the game.

'Who was that on the phone?' Maisie demands from the top of the stairs.

Liza glances at the time on the oven. 'If you're not in your uniform in the next two minutes you're not going to school.'

Maisie bolts back into her room. Liza hears floorboards creaking, footsteps rumbling down the stairs. Maisie topples into a chair and shovels a spoon of porridge into her mouth.

'Slow down, sailor,' Liza says.

'Thought we were late.'

Liza fixes the parting in Maisie's hair, combs her fingers through it. 'I thought I could take some pictures of you all smart in your uniform. With your lovely new haircut.'

'It's not the first day.'

The banana is brown sludge in the heat of the porridge.

'With Spud if you like.'

Maisie's smile is all milk teeth and silliness as she stoops over Spud.

'Cheese,' she says.

A motorbike roars past and Spud bays from her cage in the boot. Liza locks the petrol pump into the car. She raps the window with her free hand and makes kissy noises. Spud looks up at her, quiets, lies down. Without knowing why Liza buys a bunch of discount roses from the garage. She watches the seep of them in the passenger seat. The air flushes sweet every time they go over a speed bump.

'Strange how much some owners look like their pets,' Liza says, watching a man hug his terrier to his chest as he crosses the car park, short ginger beard brushing up against his dog's. Spud waggles her feet in the air as Liza lowers her to the ground. She pulls Liza towards the building and sniffs at a chihuahua tied to the railing outside.

Inside: a huge stencilled pawprint on the wall. Liza goes up to the smiling girl behind the kiosk. She gives Liza a form and a chewed biro. Liza prints her phone number in the little boxes. She scribbles out the penultimate figure. She grips the tail of the pen in her teeth before realising and spitting it back out. She sinks to her knees. Her face is warm with Spud's gravelled breath. She holds Spud's ears. She kisses her firmly on the head. She stands, hands over the leash.

'We'll let you know when we've found her new family,' the girl says.

Leaning against the jamb, Liza cannot recognise which of the cars is hers.

THE DANCE BETWEEN DARKNESS & LIGHT

JEAN ROARTY

I pretend not to notice the stares as I head to the supermarket on my electric mobility scooter. My balance is a little unsteady, so it's a godsend. I tighten my hands around the handles and resist the urge to speed up. It takes fifteen minutes if there are no bins or bikes blocking my way, or cars parked on the footpath. I turn left out of the housing complex then it's straight on all the way. I know every crack and bump on the footpath. There is a cycle lane I use sometimes, but it disappears completely just before the letterbox.

'Mam cycle lanes are for bikes,' Deirdre said when I told her.

I was housebound before I got the *Elite Traveller*. I can still walk a bit, but tire easily. It was Deirdre who brought me to the mobility shop in town. We viewed deluxe models with full suspension. Those styles came in Chartwell Green and Viking Red, but the basic black is fine. I'll never want for anything else.

To not want is what I want.

The scooter is handy when I only need a few bits. They fit into the wire basket on the front. In the shop, someone always offers to reach items that are up high, and I thank them for their act of kindness. I could get off the scooter and reach stuff myself but it's a chance to talk. I love looking at the random stuff (as Deirdre calls it) in the middle aisle but try to resist buying anything; I rely on the state pension.

I scoot in through the sliding glass doors and head down the aisles. First, I put the food I need into the basket: milk, bread and bananas. I savour the scent of fruit and the tempting aroma of freshly baked bread. Manoeuvring around the special-offer stand, I speed past the chilling bite of the freezers. Four penalty points! Finally, I linger over the middle aisle. On special offer today we have toolboxes, gym towels, cutlery, floor varnish and colouring books. I reach over and grab a colouring book. I prop it up in the basket like a windshield. Jenny will love that. I spoil her but that's what grannies do.

Last week, I foolishly put my groceries back and got a set of six screwdrivers, a lamp and an alarm clock, none of which I needed. The lamp has long spikes like blades of grass that light up. The colours change all on their own. When I stare at it, rainbow colours spiral around me as if I'm inside a kaleidoscope.

I forget about everything.

Further down the aisle I see interesting gadgets. The secateurs are tempting—I could put the bananas back. No. A man comes to do the communal garden, so that would be a waste of money.

At the checkout, I feel the stares. 'Go on ahead,' says the woman in front. I thank her over the beeping sound of items being scanned. The doors part as I approach the exit, and I set off for home. Clouds like day-old bruises gather in the sky. Luckily, I'm wearing my jacket with the hood.

As I pull away, I notice a sign glowing with defiance against the gloomy weather. 'Life Molecule', the bright letters say. I haven't a clue what that means, but underneath, in smaller letters, it says: 'Healing, Meditation and Exercise Centre'. Wow, it's just around the corner in the next building and I never noticed it before. Could this place be a way to keep my legs moving? Hope makes my decline less difficult to bear. The dance between darkness and light never goes away. I want to stand up on the scooter and shout, *Look, everybody. Look what I've found.* I scoot along the path beside the car park for a closer look passing the trolley bay with its dwindling supply of trolleys. I position myself behind a white Mini parked near the door. I had thought the space was empty until I noticed the Mini hiding between two cars, like a child among adults. From here, I watch women my age—some even older, a few men, and younger women in leggings and luminous tops go in and out. Every time the door opens, it chimes. I climb off the scooter and take an information leaflet from the plastic box beside the door. I peep in through the glass and see yellow roses on a little table. The door chimes.

'Coming in?' asks an older woman on her way out.

I hesitate. The scooter would be safe enough here and there aren't any steps. I'm dying to find out about this place.

'No. Thanks anyway,' I hear myself say. I squash the leaflet into the zippy part of my bag which I wear around me like a sash. Then I make my way back to the scooter and continue the journey home. I should have gone in. I should have made enquiries. Why didn't I? I beat myself up all the way home. I jolt over a bump; better concentrate.

As soon as I'm in the door I take out the leaflet and read it. It says the centre uses a holistic concept based on thousands of years of Chinese wisdom. It has various classes and treatments that benefit all sorts of physical and mental ailments. You pay a monthly, six monthly or annual fee to join.

A key turns in my front door. 'It's only me,' Deirdre calls out. She calls as often as she can.

'Hi Deirdre.' I shout and hurry out to the hall. With one hand on the grab rail, I shove the leaflet into Deirdre's hands. 'Read this.'

She comes in, sits on the couch with her coat still on and studies the leaflet. She's frowning and moving her head slightly from side to side. She crumples up the leaflet and tosses it on to the coffee table.

'Don't go near that place,' she says.

'Why not?'

'They could be preying on vulnerable people.'

I sag against the wall. 'It's not like I'm joining a cult.'

'Isn't that scooter enough?' She yanks her handbag out from under her and dumps it on the floor. Hanging on to the chair with one arm, I lift the crumpled leaflet from the coffee table and sit down. I place it on my thigh and rub the glossy paper over and over with my hand, smoothing out the wrinkles.

'That mobility yoke is more trouble than its worth,' she says. My grip tightens on the leaflet. Deirdre gets up and paces around the room. 'Mam, you can barely stand. How are you going to get up or down on a mat for those classes?' She takes off her coat and throws it on the couch saying she can't stay long. A stinging silence hangs in the air. It's all I can do not to cry. Deirdre gives me an anxious look. I know I annoy her, especially when I ring her at work, and she gets into trouble for taking personal calls.

'Ah Mam, I didn't mean it 'bout the scooter,' she says and goes into the kitchen. I hear her filling the kettle and banging presses. When she reappears, she gives a little self-conscious cough 'What do I know about healing centres?' she says, 'I'll buy you something to wear.'

'Don't bother.'

'Ah, Mam.'

'I'm not going.'

'No harm trying it.'

'One of your old tracksuits will do fine.'

We both smile.

'Nah' she says, shaking her head. 'You need the proper gear.'

I read out loud from the leaflet: 'Learn about Pilates, yoga, meditation—'

'Just be careful Mam. It could cost a fortune. You could get injured and end up worse.' Deirdre goes back to the kitchen and comes out with a mug in each hand. I place mine on the coffee table.

'I guess they can't all be agile if it's a healing centre.' I say. Deirdre puts her mug down and comes over and gives me a hug. 'You'll be grand, Mam.'

'With a bit of luck, the others will be worse than me.'

I book my free-trial class. I'm nervous but tell myself it will be a chance to talk to someone. Nights are hardest. In the terrifying aloneness, I find myself longing for the comfort of an arm around me. Deirdre is right about getting up and down on a mat. I hadn't thought of that. I'm also worried because I don't believe in universal energy, or ancient wisdom, or any of that stuff.

I haven't lived. I've only ever been to Lourdes, Liverpool and Bali—Ballybunion as the joke goes. I've never even had my nails painted for Christ's sake. I ache for more.

As per Chiang's instructions, I arrive early for the class. Now I'm here I don't want to go in. I'm tempted to turn around but force myself to push open the door. The chime sound jangles my nerves. I take extra care with my steps, making sure to stay close to the wall. Chiang comes out from behind the desk to greet me. He's tall and his black hair looks prickly. His wife, Lin, has beautiful long dark hair. They're both wearing navy tops and silky, bulbous trousers that come in at the ankles like something Aladdin would wear. I sit on the black leather seat and look around. The yellow roses are still going strong. Must be the healing energy. There are diagrams on the wall in Chinese script. A nearby door has a sign saying *Healing Room*. I won't be going in there; I can't be healed.

I see books on a shelf about brainwaves, chakras, meditation and meridian lines. What have I let myself in for? Chiang gives me a piece of paper with prices and times

I glance at the prices. If I stop buying silly stuff in the supermarket, I could join for a month. Chiang hands me a clipboard and pen.

I dig out my glasses and have a read. It's a questionnaire asking: name, address, date of birth, phone number, e-mail, any medical conditions etc. As I'm filling it in, the regulars arrive. They seem in good form chatting away to each other. Some sit on the black seats, others head down the corridor. I look around and smile as I hand the clipboard back.

'You new?' one of the ladies asks.

I nod. Before I have time to speak, Lin comes over with a tray of drinks in little egg cup things.

I take one.

A gong sounds. The others abandon their cups and head towards the hall. One or two are stiff and slow-moving. I let out a huge breath and follow. In the hall, Chiang bows, says something in Chinese and the class begins. We stand up and move our arms and legs copying what he is doing. I'm no worse than the others. When we use the mats, Chiang helps some of us to get back up. Soon, I'm tapping my arms, chanting, balancing my chakras, stretching my meridians, being mindful. After class I retrieve the fluorescent pink runners Deirdre got me. No need for a high-vis jacket with these. I need to sit to put them on.

'See you next time,' the arthritis lady says. The door chimes as I make my way back out to the *Elite Traveller*. This time the sound enters my body with perfect resonance.

SECOND TIME ROUND

JANE DOWNING

Her heels sank deep into the carpet, catching Chloe momentarily off balance. She reached for her mother's arm in case the older woman needed help, but her mother was better provisioned and simply planted her walking stick down more forcefully.

Mother and daughter were given little time to acclimatise from the outside chill to the warmth of the shop before an attendant offered herself, a mature woman exuding confidence and a scent unlikely to have been endorsed by a pop celebrity. Music murmured a siren song to serenity. The prices of the wedding dresses hanging down the sidewalls were discreetly marked and, once Chloe ventured to look, eye-watering.

But who, all the messaging implied, had the heart to stint on their Big Day, their heart having already been given away?

Chloe and her mother separated and addressed themselves to the selection, Chloe's mother running her hand down the sleeves of all the dresses on the white spectrum, choosing by touch, not because at eighty-one her eyesight was failing particularly, but because there were too many synthetic fabrics that sat the hairs on the back of her neck up.

Chloe loosened her woollen scarf and started on the opposite line of wedding dresses. She pulled one from the rack, noted the hanger was padded, encased in silk and fringed with lace. The hanger. Before even getting to the dress. She caught a glimpse of herself in one of the seemingly infinite number of full-length mirrors to left and right. Time had not been kind. The white cloud of fabric that went into the skirt was, in the reflection, draped over a brown, leathered arm. The reflection of the crystal chandelier thankfully obscured her face. She pulled the dress up to her chest and let it fall in mimicry of a proper try-on.

Her mother hissed at her through the perfumed air. 'Pure white is not appropriate for second weddings. White is not for old women until it's time for their funeral shroud.'

'Thanks Mum.' Chloe's sarcasm sank into the thick carpet.

Her mother stomped forward, one foot, walking stick, second foot, which helped Chloe reinsert the frippery into its space in the line of dreams. All white as virginal snow in the light streaming into the shop.

Chloe's mobile rang, interrupting the search. An unknown number. She reluctantly took the call, feeling the pressure of time—there was a lot to get through as even second weddings take a fair amount of organising. Her voice lightened when the florist introduced himself. He confirmed the lapel flowers to match the bride's bouquet. He described them as 'boutonnières.' Chloe flinched. She was pretty sure the word had never crossed her lips. What was wrong with using buttonhole? Weddings were getting more pretentious by the minute. What were they thinking…

But after the call she was able to take out her list, a crumpled, smeared piece of oft-folded A4, lean it against one of the many full-length mirrors, and cross off one more thing-to-do.

While Chloe had been busy acquiring the expensive hothouse flowers, her mother had continued addressing the first item on the dreaded list—capitalised importantly—and had made some dress choices to take to the fitting room.

'We're caught in a montage from a rom-com,' Chloe groaned after the first curtain call. The attendant, ever solicitous, nevertheless ignored the remark. Perhaps she'd heard it too many times before.

'Why did you end up deciding to get married back then?' her mother asked after three more tiring trips in and out of the changing rooms where they'd exhausted the game of remembering and sharing descriptions of wedding dresses past. The question was a bit unfair, Chloe thought, because she would never dare ask her mother the same question back.

And yet the question got her thinking. *Because I was in love*, sounded too naive at their current ages, fifty-three and eighty-one. Especially as her mother had been around for a ringside seat to her dithering. Was love ever the full answer at any age anyway?

Before she could put any adequate answer into words the attendant reappeared behind them. 'Were you thinking a hat or a veil?' she asked.

Chloe noted the size of the woman's engagement ring and the shininess of her wedding ring. As perfect as stage props.

They needed a coffee after the expedition, Chloe suggested, and her mum readily agreed. 'Do you think you can walk over to the mall?' Chloe asked. 'Or will I get the car?'

Her mother shook her walking stick like a swashbuckler's sword. 'With my trusty friend…'

They kept to the cement pavement though it would have been shorter cross-country, because they knew the perils of uneven ground. Ice frosted the grass within a trapezoid of shadow cast by the buildings, while the blades sprang up green and fresh in the province of the sunshine. The shopping mall looked positively Shangri-La like in the distance. After a few minutes, Chloe regretted not getting the car. She feared if she left her mother on the footpath to get it now, her mother would freeze into a solid block. A fine civic statue.

'Will we put a ribbon across the bonnet of the Holden?' she asked as a distraction.

'Where did all this superstitious, childish nonsense come from?' her mother sighed.

Chloe took her arm. Perhaps they'd already done too much for the day.

The mall was less Shangri-La, more something out of a sci-fi movie. A nexus of space-age effects bombarded the two women from all sides as soon as the doors slid closed behind them. Screens flashed neon advice on exercise and de-cluttering and, strangely, the therapeutic value of revisiting favourite shows and books. A huge hanging poster dominated the three storeys of the space, brightly advertising a show about the course of true love.

All the lights and noise of raw commerce were overwhelming. But at least it was warm. The tip of Chloe's nose started to tingle as feeling crept back into it. 'Here, I'll stick your gloves into the bag with mine,' she offered her mum as they stood still and proceeded downwards on the magic of the escalator.

The food court shouted with signs. Wok, wok, sushi, sushi, burger fast, fast food. One empty food outlet shadowy dark and unlit, drew Chloe's eye—a black hole—and then she was drawn back to the shiny, shiny.

The barista's smile was wide and open, quite the opposite of that of the woman at the wedding dress establishment when she'd realised which of the customers she was selling a wedding dress to. A gaping mouth quickly masked, a look of disbelieving horror lingering in the eyes. Chloe would share the reaction with her husband Michael once they were face-to-face and she could act the scene out. Together they'd relish the misunderstanding. That a woman in her 80s could be remarrying was pretty… special.

Neither she nor her mother mentioned love out loud over their thick porcelain cups, not even when the caffeine hit their bloodstreams. The wedding, unlike the marriage, was about more practical things. The list lay unfolded on the table between them. Her mother reread it again. Chloe was not listening. She was back with her mother's question at the Bridal shop: why had she agreed to marry Michael when they'd both been too *young* to know what forever meant.

It was best to forget some parts of a story: like inauspicious beginnings, like the fact that she'd not accepted Michael's first proposal, even though he'd gone down on one knee in the inconvenient snow, because it had been winter then too, and Chinese winters could get a lot colder than Australian. They'd been sightseeing and he'd unexpectedly dropped to his knee beside a rubbish bin. Which wasn't as bad as it sounded because it was a rubbish bin in a palace no less, a Chinese palace, so the bin was in the shape of a panda. Chloe still had a photo of it—the panda bin, not the proposal to which she'd said no.

The long, long journey back home she remembered as being largely, coldly, silent. She had an image of Michael walking too fast through the airport terminal, then stopping to hold the door of the taxi open for her.

'Do you remember me telling you about the time Michael proposed to me on that trip to Beijing when we'd just finished university? We were in the Forbidden City.'

'Tell it again,' her mother offered generously.

So Chloe told, over their shopping mall coffee-and-donuts. It was easier for her to do the talking when her mother was tired.

Halfway through her cobbled together narrative, she realised she'd be telling an entirely different story about her trip to Beijing if her marriage to Michael hadn't worked out. She'd be rewriting the first proposal as a harbinger of doom, not merely a false start, a small hiccough. Obviously she'd said yes eventually, the second time he'd plucked up the courage to ask, and then time and countless tides had flooded by and beached her here today, wedding dress hunting with her mother.

'I wonder what possessed him to ask me in the Forbidden City? Such a foreboding name for a place, doesn't auger well for important questions!'

Her mother snorted. Chloe was making the first, failed proposal a funny story for her because it was funny in retrospect. And by some miracle her marriage to Michael had been both long and fruitful, funny and fun. Children. Grandchildren. Their two youngest grandkids would be flower girls at their great-gran's upcoming wedding in the Botanic Gardens.

Where was Michael now, Chloe wondered, where precisely at this very moment? The A4 list had him down for organising the playlist with the DJ for the so-called wedding breakfast. 'Breakfast at six in the evening? Do we have to persist with all the wedding hoopla terminology at their age?' he'd asked earlier over their real breakfast. 'Why can't we just call it a wedding dinner? A wedding celebration if we want to be all extra special?'

The whole thing did seem unlikely, bordering on absurd, crossing the border. They'd discussed it in bed with the lights out and in the kitchen while the jug boiled and in the car while they waited for the windscreen to defrost. Discussing it through, then circling round to cover all the bases again. First, the big question of why a pair of octogenarians were up for marriage. And once they'd accepted the inevitability of it, around they went again to dissect why on earth her mother was going all out for a big wedding, one with bells and whistles.

Chloe looked across at her mother's tired face and stopped her retelling of the day in Beijing. 'Are you nervous?' she asked her mother. She remembered she'd been knotted with doubts and hesitations on her one and only wedding day.

At eighty-one, her moustache newly disappeared under peroxide treatment, her hair tightly permed and coloured, her carefully chosen wedding ensemble in a flashy cardboard bag at her feet, her mother said that, yes, she was nervous.

'You know I loved your father?' she added.

'Don't you worry about us,' Chloe said to stop her from any untoward revelations.

'Having a suitor after all this time has been exciting,' her mother confessed.

Suitor. A title from another era. But thank goodness she'd never called him her boyfriend; so wrong for anyone over eighteen let alone eighty.

'Harry does me good. Keeps me young.'

Her mother wiped the residue of a frothy cappuccino from the wrinkles at the corner of her lips and reapplied lipstick, guiding her hand with the help of her reflection in the screen of her sleeping mobile phone.

Chloe left her mother in the food court while she went to get the car and bring it to a closer park. Then together they negotiated the wind tunnel of colour-coded bays in the mall's multi-story car park, counting four ocean blue columns from the top of the escalator.

'Did you ever get to the Forbidden City?' her mother asked as they filled the boot of Chloe's sedan with bags, careful not to crush the wedding outfit and remembering to keep the last-minute box of lemon-and pansy-petal tarts flat.

Chloe kept her face down, avoiding her mother's eyes. She wondered if her story had been too convoluted in the telling twenty minutes earlier. That was not an explanation for her mother's question though. Her mother had seen the photographs when they'd got back from the trip thirty years earlier and there had long been a framed print in Chloe and Michael's lounge room, on the shelf beside the complete works of Austen.

There was only one explanation for the way her mother's memory was increasingly slipping haphazardly over the past like this. Yet she kept denying there'd been a diagnosis. Kept forgetting what the doctor had told them. Chloe and Michael had discussed that too, at length, deciding that because her mother's past was uncertain, misted, fragmented, fraught, increasingly lost in the shadows, she was right to keep looking to the future. Her wedding and her Harry were the future.

'It's a brilliant place,' Chloe said over-brightly. She held the passenger door open for her mother. She made it a rule never to call attention to her slips. 'We took the kids to the Forbidden City, when they were in high school,' she said, a tangent, an answer. Before she turned the ignition and the car's radio shouted out, deflecting the conversation elsewhere.

She remembered how loudly she and Michael had hooted on the return trip when they found a panda-shaped rubbish bin, embarrassing their children, neither able to explain why it was so funny. Some things, like love, being untranslatable.

'You've made a good choice,' she told her mother. 'You were right in the end—a dress isn't right for a winter bride. And you looked lovely in the slinky trousers and that long shirt is gorgeous. The pearly buttons down the long cuffs are special.'

'They are like snowflakes,' her mother said as they emerged out of the dingy car park and into the light.

She was not wrong. Each mother of pearl button was etched with a different geometric pattern, variations on a theme, which Chloe had described to herself as mini mandalas. A mandala: the visual representation of a journey, the soul moving from the outside down to the inner core. The most important journey in life. But it was winter now and her mother had seen them as snowflakes, and they were beautiful.

'We'll make sure they last a little longer than snowflakes,' Chloe said, mainly to reassure herself.

NO ONE TALKS ANYMORE

SEAN CRAWLEY

Noelene Anderson has no idea how so many leaves get into her house. There are flyscreens on the windows, and she keeps the front and back doors closed, but still they get in. She sweeps them up into her long-handled dustpan. Her back is not as strong as it used to be, and her knees—well, that's another story. Must make that doctor's appointment.

There's another leaf, under the dining table. How did it get there?

She calls the doctor. After listening to the menu options and pressing number 3, an automated voice says, 'Please hold while you are connected to the next available receptionist.' Tinny muzak plays. The short, annoying tune loops over and over.

'We are currently experiencing long wait times. Did you know you can make an appointment to see your doctor online? Please visit greenhillmedical dot com and click on, *Make An Appointment*, it's that easy.'

No it's not, she thinks. Just logging on to her computer is tricky enough. She hangs up.

With her hands in the sink, Noelene looks out the kitchen window. Next door's kitchen window is directly opposite. Sometimes she catches a glimpse of the tenants there. Mostly though, their blind is pulled down. She wonders if she has been caught looking. I mean, it's hard not to look. She knows nothing about these new tenants. They moved in four months ago, but she wouldn't recognise them if she bumped into them in the street. Her glimpses have been fleeting. Figures moving about or standing at the sink. She's not even sure how many live there. Maybe two, a man and a woman, but there seems to be four cars that park in the driveway or out on the street. She hopes they aren't drug dealers.

The tenants before were a family of four. A single mother and three kids. Noelene liked the chats she had with Vanessa, the mother. And she liked the sound of the two younger children, a boy and a girl, playing in their backyard. They had a trampoline and the squeals of joy put a smile on her face. The oldest of the children was a girl named Sinclair. Unusual. Apparently, she was sixteen and had an attitude. Vanessa dreaded having to teach her daughter to drive. 'She reckons she knows everything. If I correct her, oh dear, what a mouthful I cop,' said Vanessa one day. Noelene has never had a drivers licence.

In the whole time Vanessa and her family lived next door, and it must have been at least two years, Noelene never once saw Sinclair. Not even a glimpse. And she never heard her, either.

There are a lot of rentals in Noelene's street. People come and go. Transient people, no roots. Back when her house was brimming with her own children, and a husband, Noelene liked not having anything to do with the neighbours. She didn't have time for others. Family was enough. She and Bruce planted trees and shrubs around the borders; they wanted privacy for themselves and the kids, a sanctuary enclosed by greenery. It mostly worked. The lilly pillies on the eastern fence out the back did a great job of screening off the villa that had been built on every square inch of the subdivision. The bamboo they planted on that same side, the clumping variety, worked as well. But bamboo continually sheds leaves, and they end up in the house, somehow.

On the western side, the kitchen window side, whatever they planted there never worked. Bruce reckoned there must have been something dumped in the soil way back when there was no garbage service in the area. He and Noelene had certainly dug up all sorts of things over the years. Bottles, broken ceramics, chunks of fibro and plaster, old paint cans, a rusty differential from a car, you name it.

The very first time Noeline did the washing up after they bought the house, she pointed out the view to Bruce.

'I'll plant a camellia there. That should block it out. And the flowers in winter will be a treat.' Bruce always had a solution. But the camellia wouldn't grow. 'I think the soil might be too sweet for a camellia. I'll put in a hibiscus. That should do.' But it, too, struggled and remained stumpy. Bruce planned to try some natives next, but then he got cancer.

The kids are long gone now. One's in the city, one moved to Queensland and the other's in England. They were twelve, ten and eight when their father died. Noelene, to this day, has no clear idea on how his wasting away and painful death affected the children. It all happened so quickly. One day here, the next gone – gone forever.

After Bruce died, she had to work long hours at a local aged care facility just to pay the bills. Yet she still couldn't afford to buy the children the brands of clothes they wanted, or the latest gadgets that every other kid reportedly possessed, and they could no longer afford to go on holidays. And when they turned sixteen, they had to get part-time jobs to pay for things like driving lessons. They hated that, the jobs, and the fact that she, unlike every other mother, didn't own a car. She wonders if that is why they have all gone away.

She rarely talks to any of them, let alone sees them. None of them could make it home last Christmas. Of course, there were travel restrictions, still, each of them seems to have adopted other families, the families of their spouses. She hardly knows the grandchildren.

After sweeping up all the leaves in the house she makes herself a cup of tea. She turns on the radio and sits down at the dining table. There is a conversation going on between Richard Fidler, whom she just loves, and some doctor. They are talking about geriatric depression. Though the subject matter may well be relevant to Noelene, it is the warm sound of the two male voices in conversation that washes over her—soothes her.

I'm going to book a flight to Queensland. I want to see my son, she thinks.

She calls the airline only to encounter a set of confusing messages and menu options. She listens to all seven options and then forgets the number she should have pressed. She hangs up.

I'll ring Katey, she thinks. She's booked for me before. She knows how to get online and do it.

'Mum, you can't ring me at work,' says Katey, 'I've told you before, these days you have to text before you call. Gotta go. Talk later. Love you.'

Noelene bites her lip. She'd forgotten this *texting before calling* rule. Katey and the others get so frustrated with her. Once, they all chipped in and bought her a computer for her 70th birthday. Katey delivered it and tried to teach her the basics: how to get online, emailing, and how to book flights. It was in vain. Not only was she struggling to learn new things, even things like cooking a lunch seemed to be becoming difficult for her. 'There's a computer class down at the Senior Citizens Club. Maybe you could go there and see them about it,' said Katey.

'I'm not joining the Senior Citizens.'

'Why not?'

'It's just a bunch of old people.'

Katey rolled her eyes. 'I have to go, Mum. I've got to get the kids ready for the school week.'

In the late afternoon, Noelene heads off for a walk by the lake. Her daily walk is gradually shrinking in length. All those years as an aged care worker have taken their toll. Katey's probably right, she thinks. I should join the senior cits. I can't pretend anymore that I'm not old. It all just went so quickly. And I shouldn't be upset that I'm all alone with the kids so far away. They are all so independent and competent. Each one a success. They have their own lives to live. They don't need me, and I shouldn't need them. I can't have expectations.

Nowadays, she makes it as far as a bench seat that is positioned in an opening carved out from the fringe of casuarinas. There is a spectacular view across the water to the hills in the distance. Here she can rest her bones, before she heads home and gets a start on dinner.

Today, a young woman is sitting on the bench seat. Noelene thinks twice about taking her usual rest. But then, the woman is seated up one end of the bench, there's room for another bum. Besides, her grinding hips need a break.

The woman is sitting cross legged on the bench. Her back is straight, and the backs of her hands are laid flat on her knees. Her fingers are making OK signs. There is an engagement ring. Her eyes are closed. She has a tightly controlled platinum blonde ponytail that arcs out from the crown of her head and these odd looking white things stuck in her ears. A phone is strapped to her upper arm. She is wearing a yellow crop top and blue floral leggings. A pair of runners with fluoro stripes sit underneath the bench.

In contrast, Noelene's hair is unruly and grey. Her slacks, blouse and cardigan are of muted tones. Her shoes are brown Hush Puppies with orthopaedic inserts.

Noelene sits down as far away as possible and as quietly as she can. But the woman senses her presence and opens her eyes. 'Sorry,' says Noelene. 'Don't mind me. Just catching my breath. I won't bother you, Dear.'

The young woman uncrosses her legs and stands up, facing Noelene, hands on hips. 'Are you kidding,' she says. 'Can't you see I was meditating. Don't you understand what that means? It means I want to be left alone.'

Noelene shrinks and shrugs. 'Sorry. I'll go,' she says and begins to shuffle her way into position so she can stand and leave.

'Jesus Christ!' The woman sits back down and reaches for her shoes. 'Forget it. It's no use now.' She slips on her socks and shoes and tugs hard at the laces. 'You Boomers have no idea what it's like. You have all day to do whatever it is you do. I commute every day to the city for uni. It's not like your day when you could get a job straight out of high school. I need this time out.'

'Yes of course. Silly of me. Sorry.'

The woman stands up and takes a last look at Noelene. She tuts and runs off.

Oh dear, says Noelene to herself. The hardest thing is how much this woman looks and sounds like her Katey.

With the young woman gone and no one else around, Noelene calls out, 'Fucking bitch!'

A big dinner doesn't suit Noelene's constitution. Tonight, she's having some soup and a slice of toast with butter. On the telly a group of women are talking about the gender pay gap. They seem so angry and demanding. Noelene doesn't understand much of what is said. It's just background chatter, really. After Bruce died, she made a concession to her three children. OK, she said, we can watch telly while we have dinner. She smiles remembering this. The kids scoffing down their dinner in a tenth of the time it took to prepare and cook and laughing at the shows they liked to watch.

The home phone rings.

'Hello?'

'Mum, it's Daniel.'

'Oh, Daniel! What a lovely surprise. How are you, my darling?'

'I'm great, Mum. Hey listen, I can't talk long, but Katey rang me just now. We're going to have Christmas up at my place. We want to fly you up. You can stay in the guest room, and Katey and her mob are going to book a cabin down by the beach at Mudjimba. She said you could stay a night or two with her and her family there as well. What do you reckon?'

'Oh Daniel, that would be lovely. You've made my day. If only Lisa could be here with us as well.'

'Yeah, she'll be freezing her arse off in London. Sucked in. But don't worry, we'll Facetime her.'

Even though she has absolutely no idea what face time is, Noelene laughs. Then, she spots a leaf under the telephone table.

6
THE LAND
DAWN **TO DUSK**

YANGGARDA YANGGARDA
LONG LONG TIME AGO

DR CHELINAY GATES

'Yanggarda... Yanggarda[1]... Long long time ago, when kangaroos walked on their tippy-tippy toes and the world was flat and kookaburras had no reason to laugh. Little hairy brown men with big ears and noses lived in huge dirt mounds, far far away from where the deadly red dirt meets the sparkling blue sea.'

'We call 'em little hairy fellas Mangawarri.[2] They turn up all excited like with their big faces smiling and twinkling goggly eyes and steal your little baby right out of your arms... sometimes even before its first cry.'

Recognising her voice, I turned to see my great grandmother sitting on the edge of our beloved waterhole... our sacred Jila.[3] She was dangling her tired old feet in the cool clear water at Dragon Tree Soak, in the middle of the Great Sandy Desert. Waving her hand at me to come sit beside her. She didn't stop to greet me but instead continued, 'Them Mangawarri[2] take ya jinjamarda[4]... ya little baby... right up high to that brightest bundara[5] – star – in the early morning sky... That's the place!' She said, pointing her long bony black finger at a star that sparkled like a diamond on a lavender sea.

'Only them pure ones can go up there.'

Then grabbing my hand real tight she took a long deep breath and turned to faced me.

'Nah... you and me can't go up there... we gotta learn the hard stuff, right down here on Country.' Leaning back, she patted the red dirt with her open hand.

'On that there Morning Star, the Great Spirits learn 'em *little ones* how ta fix 'em *up everythin'*... How put all them *wrong things... the right way around* again. Then those *little babies* fly back down to earth to find us fellas... the *Julgia*[6]... *broken ones*. They don't want to see ya feelin' sorry for ya self. Gently, gently they make us strong and *straighten up* us fellas' thinking. So that we can do what we gotta do... All them right things... In the proper way.'

Note: Indigenous Languages. Wajarri from the Pilbara and Mangala from The Great Sandy Desert.
[1] Yanggarda Yanggarda: long long time ago (Wajarri)
[2] Mangawarri: little hairy brown men that live in mounds (Wajarri)
[3] Jila: waterhole (Mangala)   [4] Jinjamarda: little baby (Wajarri)   [5] Bundara: star (Wajarri)
[6] Julgia: broken, a word my dad used don't know what language

Suddenly I felt the sodden earth beneath my bum give way and I fell into the sacred Jila[3]. Jalbri shouted after me... 'Balayi! Balayi![7] ... Look out! Look out!'

'Them little ones will make you laugh when you really want to cry.' My quivering lips turned reluctantly into a sad smile. 'I've even seen 'em little ones bring on the rain, in the middle of the desert on a stinkin' hot day.' Lowering her voice she said... 'And you'll find yourself swimming in a waranggu[8] (rainbow) just when you think you're gonna die.'

At that moment a waranggu-coloured oil slick surrounded me and I went under. 'Grandma!' I yelled... 'I'm scared!' 'Hey girl, don't you be worrying. Them jinjamarda[4] are givin' ya sign that they're lookin' out for ya...' her voice trailed off... 'you're not alone.'

Slowly, so slowly I drifted down deep into the warm oily green water, at Dragon Tree Soak. Turtles circled around and around me, nipping my fingers and toes. Suddenly, those tickles turned into terror as I remembered how those same turtles had cleaned my dead grandma's bones. An icy current curled it's fingers around me... 'Don't go!' I screamed in bubbles, that only I could hear *pop*, as I watched them make their way to the surface.

All the while *the darkness* dragged me down to where them *little babies'* shadows, don't ever go.

Suddenly the watery-ness disappeared, replaced by air that seemed thick and heavy on the skin. I struggled to breathe. Then the side of my right foot made contact with the cold hard concrete floor. Staggering forward I fell heavily to my knees... I knew exactly where I was.

Hearing footsteps approaching the prison door I quickly dragged myself back to my mattress on the floor in the corner of the cell. Tucking the filthy pillow under my head I laid there pretending to be invisible. But I couldn't take my eyes off a little flower made of freshly knotted grass... my hand shot out... I grabbed the little flower and pressed it to my lips. I closed my eyes and deeply inhaled that sweet grassy smell like lovers do down by the riverbed. Then I shoved the twined treasure under my pillow.

'C'mon little Petal.' Lookin' up I saw a skinny old woman with snow-white hair sitting in front of me blackfella style... bum down and knees out. But Delores Flower had died years ago.

'Somethin' bothering you girl?' Her blue eyes sparkled like a waterhole on a hot summer's day. 'Remember what I told ya 'bout string? Over and under... in and through... then pull it all together. That's all ya need ta know to make ya life good.'

Just as I was about to speak, she raised her long bony black finger to her lips... gave a gentle wave and in the next breath she was gone. But from the small, barred window high on the prison wall, the light catching the dust was strangely rainbow hued.

My jinjamarda[4] kicked inside my womb... and I knew for sure that I was not alone.

Note: Indigenous Languages. Wajarri from the Pilbara and Mangala from The Great Sandy Desert.
[1] Yanggarda Yanggarda: long long time ago (Wajarri)
[2] Mangawarri: little hairy brown men that live in mounds (Wajarri)
[3] Jila: waterhole (Mangala)   [4] Jinjamarda: little baby (Wajarri)   [5] Bundara: star (Wajarri)
[6] Julgia: broken, a word my dad used don't know what language
[7] Balayi: watch out (Wajarri)   [8] Waranggu: rainbow (Wajarri)

CLEAR WATER

LEONE GABRIELLE

one blackberry arm dips
languid into the stream

this is your place
your last place
i crouch the earth is wet

your bones
the little crab hill of you has flattened
rust drifts over your shimmer

i catch me in your blue handkerchief
that i think i shall never wash

i know the heavy shale
is your bones
your spine your skull
that you shall never be as you were
that i am forever changed

the dog leaps over bracken
nosing me to move on
soon i won't see your pieces

i get up
walk slowly back
pick a dry track across rivulets
between the willows
you planted

i stand still
in the bouquet of swamp
up high the top branches buzz
last sun illuminates yellow toothed leaves
reaching forward

TWILIGHT OF A SEASON

BROOKS CARVER

The fields were quiet after harvest was done. It was November. As we plodded along, my golden retriever breathed in the likely pheasant scents, those faint, elusive clues hidden in the pasture grass. The horizon was blurred with light rain at the tree line where Little Indian Creek plunged into my stretch of woods. We walked the timber's edge, and I checked the old growth for deer. A small herd lived there. I could spare what little grain they needed as they frequently feed in my cornfields. Occasionally, they peered out at me from the deep woods, and I gazed back at them. They were safe, safer than they could know. My dog spooked one from time to time. Away they both went, across the fields and over the hills, but my hunter returned to me after a few minutes. She was fast in her younger days, but not that fast. The deer always came back later when we had left.

I remember other hunts in other seasons with my sons-in-law, serious hunters all. The dog was in her prime then, leading the way. Pheasants burst noisily into the sun and silhouetted against the sky as they climbed hard on strong, autumn-colored wings. In those days, with the three boys, I never carried a gun, content to work the dog, watching her instinctive, outstanding skills. We always came home near the limit. November hunts. Good, long ago, shiny, bright autumn days.

In later years, when my Golden was gray of the muzzle and had eyes that held such knowledge, we hiked rather than hunted. We kidded each other into pretending it was a hunt because I took my shotgun along, but we both knew better. I let her run free. She ranged as far ahead as she wished, and when she flushed a bird, I think she understood why I didn't shoot. We had harvested enough birds through the years. We had our memories. Enough was enough. The dog sometimes vanished far ahead out of range, but I knew she waited for me under the old-growth cottonwood that spread its limbs over the creek like a blessing. It was our spot to stop and rest. I sat down among the roots, rested my head against the trunk, and breathed in the fragrance of the nearby woods. She stared intently at my jacket pocket for a time, focused and anxious to eat. We shared a granola bar. Afterward, she waded into the creek, drank deeply, and checked out muskrat and raccoon scents. The stream, never trapped, had a large population. Then it was time for us to move on, our ritual completed.

Twilight came unexpectedly on that rainy November afternoon, with only a slight darkening of an already dark sky. Winter loomed just beyond the rain. As the temperature dropped, the light rain turned to wet snow. The wind calmed, and the land was still except for a faint hissing of flakes falling through the nearby trees. It became a black-and-white world. A lone pheasant exploded from his brushy hiding place, unexpected to us both. I fired a shot, deliberately wild, just once more to hear the sound. It was a celebration of sorts, I guess. The report echoed across the waterways and pastures, down through the timber and valleys we have hunted so many times. The bird flew down the passageway between the trees and vanished into a moody sky, free to die by other means during the harsh winter or live yet another year. The air grew still—snowflakes danced and swirled. I tipped back my head, and the snow touched my face and lightly melted there. I watched the breath stream from my mouth and disappear.

The night began to descend, and it was time to head for home. Not far. Fog rolled into the bottoms. We followed a fence line for a mile or so, then walked south on our country road. A neighbor drove by, truck headlights glowing through the flurries and near darkness. I wave to him, and he did the same. We talked for a moment about crop prices, weather, and birds, and then he drove away, taillights vanishing into the gloom and snow. The sound of his tires on gravel faded in the muffled darkness. The dog and I walked past the pine grove at the edge of the yard and towards the welcoming kitchen light that spilled onto the wet, snow-covered leaves—no birds to clean tonight.

I shucked my boots by the door, toweled off the dog, and stepped into the warmth and fine cooking smells of supper. My hunter took a drink of water, circled twice over her rug in front of the register, plopped down with a deep sigh, and immediately fell asleep. She snored with a soft buzz. Her gray muzzle rested between huge, rough front paws. Her life was simple and unadorned. She dreamed her dreams of hunts on smoky, crisp autumn mornings, fetching sticks on the lake, and riding in the truck, wherever old dog dreams took her.

There was nothing remarkable about any of it, yet somehow there was. The world turned over slightly, and I wished that soft, snowy November afternoon, so full of grace, had never ended.

MIND FISH

JENIFER HETHERINGTON

My last visit to the dam was in
lush November, now a harsh autumn

crack-crazed mud in the shallows
crumble dry banks

I sit, hope for darts of gold,
of gilt stippled charcoal

sleek flip of feather fin swishing
in limpid green.

Today, milky tea water,
riffled by chill wind

only mind fish in view,
they are enough.

Thoughts soar with black cockatoos
calling in flight between tall trees

laughter ricochets—kookaburras
sentinel at forest edge—

mind skitters, plummets to
the absence of gold shimmer

those birds don't belong—
thoughts spike

neither do we
nor the fish

they stir up the sand bed,
stripped the muddy banks bare.

A glint deep under the surface,
serried row of gleaming bars—

these are no mind fish—
then I see you

had forgotten the lustrous
flip of white feather tail

single band of pale amber where tail
thickens, becomes body—

your glistening twin glides
into view at bank's edge

a waterborne mirror dance
in murky shallows—

now hidden again
below the rock where I sit—

thoughts arising, disappearing—
you are mind fish again.

THE TASTE OF LAND

FRANÇOISE THORNTON-SMITH

Jane heard a metallic sound: a key in a lock, a squeaky metal door. She turned her head slightly to hear better. He was taking a gun from the firearms cabinet. Something jangling—the cartridges from the lower drawer. How many did he take?

She looked up from the trousers she was mending.

'I'm off to the southern paddock. The header's still OK. Shouldn't take all day.' Luke put on his worn, sweat-stained cap and patted his shirt pocket for his cigarettes.

'You want me to come with you? Do you want a thermos of tea and a sandwich?' She put her hands on the table to push herself up.

Luke waved at her to sit down again. 'She's right. I've got water. I'll call you on the UHF if I want something.' He took his cap off again and rubbed his forehead. He went into the dark hallway. She heard footsteps, the flywire door squeak and close. She heard the ute start up and leave.

Why take the gun if you're out on the header? Why bother harvesting if it's worthless anyway? Why bother? She looked down at the worn trousers in her hands. Why be a farmer? Why be a farmer's wife?

A few minutes later, Jane opened the flywire door. She stood on the veranda in the glaring sunshine and watched the dust from Luke's ute settle on the gravel track. The chickens needed feeding. Jane scanned the dried-out lawn for snakes. She had stopped watering the lawn last summer. She had stopped watering her roses and dahlias the summer before. She would prefer to walk with her eyes closed; not see her home crumbling around her. Her straw hat protected her skin, but she felt blackened within. When she and Luke had married and she moved out here, the whole farm had been green and lush. It was a fertile, productive place, where things could be made to happen. She had flowers and fruit trees and chickens, and Luke rejoiced in them too. She didn't care now. She wanted Luke to stop pretending things would come good. He was pretending, wasn't he? There was nothing here for them anymore. It was a parched, bleak place of no beauty. Even Luke's beloved Grampians had burned.

The feed bin in the chook shed was newly filled with wheat: last week's harvest from the 40-acre block. Jane was amazed anything had come off it. Luke said he couldn't sell that wheat, but it would do as chicken feed. 'The wheat's no good, even without all the stones and twigs. The land is letting me down,' he had said, turning his head away and leaning on the shed doorpost. 'Or I'm letting the land down. I don't know.' Jane wanted to touch him. He left the shed before she could.

Jane filled the water trough. She looked around. The chook yard used to be the orchard as well. She had stopped watering the trees three years ago. Only one fruit tree was still alive, hanging on through the years of drought. How could a soft stone fruit like the apricot withstand the onslaught of heat, strong northerlies and lack of water? Yet here it was, not only alive but laden with fruit. When she looked around at the remains of her garden, Jane felt angry towards that tree. It should just keel over as well. Join the rest. Everything dead, black, a clean ending.

The chickens scratched the dusty earth around her feet, seeking the grain she had scattered. She did like her chooks. She put a hand on a branch of the apricot and stared vacantly at the massive ridge line of the Grampians in the distance. Luke had taken her hiking there, fifteen years ago. She had loved the bush then, like he did. She had loved the farm too, like he did. She had loved Luke then. Not anymore? She dug her fingernails into the branch, and remembered the perfume of the apricot blossom. The luscious fruits and green leaves hung around her. Jane shook the branch angrily. An apricot fell off. The hens immediately ran over and pounced on it, ripping into the succulent flesh with their beaks and claws. Jane watched, entranced. She picked an apricot from the tree and checked it for blemishes or insects. It was perfect. She held it to her nose and closed her eyes and then bit into it. Juice dribbled down her chin. Bliss, she thought. She laughed out loud, half bitterly, half happily. I have to tell Luke about the apricots. And I can make an apricot pie. With more spring in her step, she left the yard, banging the gate shut behind her as usual. Twigs fell off the dead grapevine entwined in the fence: dry, brittle fingers letting go and giving up. And yet not all is lost, Jane told herself. She stamped over the crackling lawn back to the dusty farmhouse, thinking of apricots and eggs, flour, sugar and milk. She would create something light and delicious and beautiful from this land. She would give Luke a taste of his land. Of their land.

'G'day Luke.' Joe leaned his arm on the window of his ute. His right arm was exceedingly brown. He spent a lot of time in his ute.

Luke pulled the hand brake on and turned the engine off. He looked further down the road, to the header he could just make out in the shimmering distance, in the southern paddock. He sighed. He leaned his brown arm on his ute window. The swirling dust settled around and on the two vehicles in the middle of the dirt road. It gently dusted the men's arms and added to the greyness of the surrounding countryside. The paddocks were bare or carried a meagre, straggly crop.

'G'day Joe. Not out on your paddock?'

'Went to see Stoner. He wants to buy a header. I'm thinking of getting rid of mine. It doesn't get much use.'

'You're not harvesting anything then?'

'Nope. I put the sheep on the big paddock. Not worth harvesting. Not worth nothing.' Joe cleared his throat and looked away for a moment.

Luke nodded. They sat there silently for a moment, looking through their dusty windscreens. They each saw their own wasted paddocks. Hungry sheep. Empty dams.

Luke cleared his throat. 'I'm harvesting the barley.'

'You're mad.'

'I put it in; I'll harvest it too.'

They shook hands, one brown arm extended out the window to the other. Joe drove off first.

Luke stopped the ute at the paddock gate and sat for a while. The dust settled. He looked at his watch. It didn't really matter. The harvesting wouldn't take him long. He stuck to the routine. He was a farmer. He sniffed the dust on his forearm and then licked it. The taste made him pause before he drove through the gate.

Four hours later he switched the header off. This lot wouldn't fill one field bin. The paddock was even barer now. Hardly worth the effort to put sheep on it for the stubble. The deep cracks in the baked earth were more visible. You could put a foot wrong, slip down into the hard, dark hole and break your leg. And there was the big old red gum in the middle of the paddock, forcing him every time to create curves in his furrows, turn while harvesting, lose precious grain because he had to cross lines despite trying to steer along the same tracks. His father had taught him how to slip the clutch on the machines and steer more smoothly around the tree. His grandfather had used horse and plough around it. Luke wouldn't get rid of the tree. It was a survivor, at least five hundred years old. It had been there before white man arrived, when this area was all forest. It must know some history. It was his family's history too. It was so alive. It was also good shelter for his stock against the sun, when his sheep were on the paddock. Luke could live with a crooked cropping line.

He climbed down from the header and walked slowly back to the ute. Somehow it was seven o'clock. Jane hadn't called him on the radio. He hadn't called her. He thought of the firearm he had taken from the gun cabinet. He thought of clean endings, but also of his land. He had faith in his land, in the soil.

The land was in him. This drought would break, and the cycle would start over. The cement-hard, dry soil would soften with rain, the cracks would fill, it would be fertile again and produce wonderful crops. Just a bit of rain. A bit of patience. He bent down and picked up a handful of dirt. He tasted it and shook the rest from his fingers. Again, the taste made him pause, stirring life into a very slight hope. He had been watching the native birds; they told him how the landscape and the climate were doing. Hope never killed a person.

Luke lit a cigarette and looked out towards the mountains, where the colours shifted and changed on the stark rock faces and charred hillsides. The bushfire last year had been a monster. He had gone out with the volunteer fire brigade on those frantic callouts, suffered from the heartache of friends' places burned down, coughed from the stench of dead animals and the smoke that hung around for months afterwards. That smoke, though, had created amazing sunsets and sunrises. And the burnt mountainsides had a special quality; they reminded him of paintings. The mountains were charcoal now, with that charcoal colour. He laughed at himself. What did he know about beauty, or art, or light or atmosphere? He didn't even talk about those things with Jane; why was that? When they married, she had been keen to become what she thought was a proper farmer's wife. All their conversations had been about farming, animals, crops, vegetables, chooks. Her chooks. Yet they had been happy. Now they never seemed to talk.

A slight twang made him look at the fence. A fox!

Luke stubbed the cigarette out between thumb and finger and reached through the open window for the gun. The cartridges were in his pocket. He loaded the gun silently. He closed the breech gently, keeping his eyes on the fox. The animal trotted confidently in the open over the harvested ground, in the light, without a care. It was a beautiful fox: rich russet red, full tail, no mange. It was a copper wave flowing over the stark stubble. Luke stepped towards the front of the ute and leaned on the bonnet. The weak rusty patch squeaked. The fox paused, turned its head and ran in the same instant.

'Damn.'

'Shit.'

Luke shook his head at his own stupidity. The fox was running towards the old gum, the only source of protection in that big bare paddock. Luke took off after it, still shaking his head, holding his gun out from him, pointing down. His footsteps thudded dully on the dry soil. Clouds of dust burst up at every step. Suddenly he had to cough violently.

'Smoking. No good.' He put the gun down and leaned over, his hands on his knees. He thought about Jane telling him to stop smoking, to wear a broad-brimmed hat, to take food with him, to take breaks. To give her a call. He thought about how Jane was unhappy here now. He knew. After a moment he picked up the gun and started moving again. He didn't run; he walked fast.

Here he was at the tree. But where was the fox? He would have seen it if it had run further. Even when he rested for a moment, he had been looking around for it. It must be at the tree.

He knew all the trees on his land and this was his favourite, despite the crooked cropping lines. Its trunk spread out widely, with dead sections and long root spurs you could trip over. Luke saw the traces of rabbits. He walked slowly around the trunk, holding his gun ready to shoot. Surely the fox would have dug itself in at the base somewhere. No fox. Luke took his cap off and scratched his head.

The low sun created a glorious atmosphere: yellow, red and violet on the tree, with the Grampians forming a vivid purple backdrop. The grey dust of his paddock had become a voluptuous, velvety claret. The stubble stalks were rods of gold. The warm air caressed his arms, which were no longer plain sunburnt brown, but burnished copper, skin of a god. Luke heard a kookaburra in the distance; for the rest it was quiet and peaceful. He stood at the base and his gaze moved up the trunk, to the branches extending out above him, the narrow gum leaves gleaming in that special light.

The fox was sitting on a wide branch about five metres up, not even looking at him. It faced the setting sun, eyes closed, enjoying the warmth. Luke slowly let out the big breath he had taken when he noticed the fox. He swung his right arm in a silent fluid movement and crooked his head into the gun. He barely breathed now. He had the fox in his sight.

The fox raised its head even further. What a beautiful animal. It stood up and stretched on the branch. So graceful. Luke closed his eyes for a moment. It was a clever fox, climbing a tree like that. Up there, it was not a piece of vermin on his land; it was a noble animal, a glorious picture. He opened his eyes and drank in the beauty of it.

The fox sat down again, basking in the last golden rays of sunlight. The sun was sinking. The ground had returned to its grey and dusty state. The only colour now was that magnificent fox there, up in the magnificent ancient tree, all aglow in that warm crimson light.

Luke lowered the gun. He shook his head and grinned wryly. He turned around and walked back to the ute. He didn't look back. The gun was heavy and useless in his hand; he felt inclined to let it drag along through the dirt. Why had he taken it with him?

When he got back to the farmhouse he would tell Jane about the wonderful fox, about the stunning colours and the painterly quality of the landscape. How his drought-stricken paddock had momentarily been a baroque carpet against a vermilion backdrop. Maybe he should take her out to the paddock one evening, so she could see the transformation. Did it happen every evening? He would like to talk with her about the taste of soil too. Give her a taste of his land. Of their land.

THIS WAY NOW

K. JANE MAY

Reluctantly Alena had left him there—left them, she prefers to think of it, in any case the *them* that she cherishes most. Unlike that otherwise so similar day last summer, when they'd picnicked beneath the blue of never-ending prairie sky, clouds had gathered, swiftly and unexpectedly as any wildlife will, seemingly out of nowhere. Yet dark and ominous as the sky had grown, it had provided the answer she'd been unable to find all the while the late afternoon sun was lighting up the ruins of that long-abandoned farmstead, when the soft breeze had arrived like an old friend, slowly and gently relieving her of her precious burden. Maybe she would have come to the same decision anyway: what, after all, was left for her out there on the Pacific coast? But she still isn't accustomed to making life-altering decisions without Hamish's input, and as she'd pulled out of the long, winding lane—towering weeds rustling between deep, rapidly muddying ruts—onto the only slightly better bumpy graveled road, fat raindrops were streaking rivers down the dusty windshield, rivaling the salty streams already ravaging her face. But it had felt okay, she acknowledges with a sense of relief. Good even, because she had made the decision. By the time she arrives in Sagebluff, the sky is black, the storm in full swing.

The little '60s rancher sits in darkness, but Alena can see by the sporadic flashes of lightning and the strobe-like beams emitted from a swaying branch-eclipsed streetlight that the yard, though neglected over many months, scarcely needs mowing; just a few scattered branches lay waiting for gathering and in deference to tidy Hamish she will make a point of doing that sooner, rather than later as per her natural wont. After inserting the key into the wobbly lock, she takes a long, deep breath before flipping the light switch just inside the door of the enclosed back porch. Her heart somersaults anyway at the unexpected familiarity; there on a row of coat hooks next to the kitchen entrance rests the stud-banded straw hat Hamish—never comfortable around hats of any sort—had been too embarrassed to wear, next to the gauzy, multi-coloured Indian scarf she never left the house without those hot, windy days. She remembers placing them there just before they locked the door late last September, thinking how those gaudy protectors would be there to greet them the following summer (and so they too cheerfully are), hopeful that Hamish might finally be persuaded to take the hat—the best she'd been able to find in the limited tiny town—with him on his prolonged hillside wanderings. Though he'd always set out so very early, he tended to get distracted, and by the time he returned, camera over shoulder, pockets bulging, the sun would be on fire, his scalp red beneath the increasingly thinning white.   She shakes her head, smiles at the memory of his inexplicable bashfulness at an age where most had become so unapologetically brash; it wasn't as if anyone saw him on those solitary adventures. She ascends the two steps that lead to the kitchen, turning on all the lights as she goes, marvels at her otherwise addled self for having had the forethought to contact the various utility companies well in advance, just in case.

They'd spent only a few months here after making the rather spontaneous purchase early last summer, and yet, as with the borrowed farmyard, the house greets her with casual warmth; it's as if she'd just stepped out for an hour or two, as opposed to returning after a nine-month absence. She isn't sure what she'd expected, but it hadn't been anything like this overwhelming, almost mocking, familiarity. She hadn't, of course, hoped for something unsavoury to deal with—a racoon infiltration say, or a leaked water pipe—but some minor catastrophe (a mouldy refrigerator, a bug infestation in the cupboards, but no, no excess bugs and the stick they'd left in the fridge door had held) would have been a welcome distraction, given her something to *deal* with. Anything but this renewed sense of loss that insists on shadowing her every step as she makes her way through the one-summer home they'd planned to make permanent. Of course, she is only five minutes in, but everything seems excruciatingly in good order. Already she sees the futility of thinking she could have left Hamish so peacefully behind in that farmyard. Left them. *They*. There. Alena knows it must be this way now. *Her*. Here.

She will forgive herself; these things, as they say, take time. Relax, she tells herself, do something normal, never mind the late hour, sleep will be impossible anyway. She'll make a pot of coffee or a cup of tea. Anything. She fumbles with the light switch beneath the shelf over the kitchen sink, and when the flickering fluorescent tube finally washes its ghostly pale yellow-green haze over the windowsill, she gasps. There, on the wooden ledge, an assortment of stones, of various shapes and sizes, colourful markings like ancient paintings in hues of terra cotta and purple dusk, fossilised wood, imprints of ancient leaves, their eerie shadows spilling over her, into her, as they creep across the cool tiled floor. She'd forgotten. Things he'd bring home from his excursions, excited over his findings the way a small boy is. A gopher's skull, sun-bleached to white. *Would it be okay if I put this here, Leni? Will it bother you?* It will bother her. *Of course you can put it there Hamish.*

She makes a strong pot of coffee, the way they both like it, and after it's brewed she pours a cup. At least she hasn't poured two cups, added sugar to one before remembering; she'd gotten past that last winter, once the sugar had finally run out. She sits down at the kitchen table, a sturdy oak too large for the space, but it had been left in the house, along with four matching chairs. She tries not to notice the emptiness of the one opposite her, the one with the lime green and orange striped cushion but that only attracts an even lonelier thought: the bed will need making up, with freshly laundered sheets. She hopes she can figure out which hoses to connect in the basement, that the old washing machine will behave—though if not, it could well provide the distraction she'd craved. But she's suddenly weary, in no hurry for dealing with anything like that; she'll just wrap herself in her fuzzy traveling blanket for tonight, curl up on the lumpy couch. She sips her coffee slowly as she surveys her surroundings. She closes her eyes.

Saskatchewan—sandwiched as it was between the provinces of their respective upbringings—had, last summer, been a return of sorts for both of them. Hamish had found something of the vanished Alberta of his youth in the vast open rangeland, the endless rolling hills with their craggy outcrops, the deep mysterious coulees dense with black poplar and wolf willow, refuge of coyotes and badgers and deer. For Alena, images of her Manitoba upbringing burned deep into her very skin: intense as the blistering hot sun were those days spent bumping along gravel roads, dodging curious transmuting gophers—one moment dignified sentries cautiously observing them from their stations along the baked-clay roadsides, the next moment frivolous, darting pups. And still in Saskatchewan, to her delight, surrounded by endless fields of wheat and barley and mustard, the quintessential wooden grain elevators and so many abandoned clapboard barns and farmhouses that drew her, trancelike. She had constantly asked Hamish to pull over somewhere so she could wander a bit, wrap herself in the allure of yesteryear she'd barely glimpsed in childhood; sure she would find the spirit of her grandparents even in the faded grey remnants of some other family's vanished past. Hamish had always indulged her, though he preferred the unspoiled beauty of a canyon, a valley too deep and rugged to have ever been cultivated. Prehistoric remnants, nature of any sort; he was not the sort of artist to get excited about old leaning barns or rusty tractors. Alena, on the other hand, marveled at the endurance of an early iron cook stove, a forgotten baby's cradle with faded stenciled rabbits, the possibilities of a sagging wraparound porch. What had their lives been like, she couldn't help but wonder about the people—particularly the women—who had once inhabited these vanished worlds.

Perhaps a happy farmwife once reigned over this domain, adored by her husband until the end; maybe a lonely war bride once sat in this kitchen—worn linoleum lifted and thick now with animal droppings, a long empty birds' nest nestled amongst the remaining shards of glistening window glass lining the sill like jewels reflecting the morning sun—writing letters, as the bread dough lay rising, to faraway friends and distant cousins who never write back, husband silent and brooding since the day tragedy struck. After a moment of silence, she would whisper a reverent farewell to the long gone mistress of the home she'd intruded upon, wipe a tear for her inevitable fate. She'd wander back outside then, look for Hamish, find him pondering badger holes, examining coyote scat; wondering at the surrounding hills and the million year old secrets that lay hidden beneath rings of cracked white mud and dark seams of coal. For Hamish, no interest at all in vulgar humanity's remains.

Until their discovery that late June afternoon, after a drive that had begun to feel disturbingly without end. Their destination undetermined after locating a barely imperceptible turnoff from the gravel road they'd been on, they had navigated a barely maintained, snaking dirt track seemingly for hours until finally it petered out. And there it was, an enchantment of an old farmstead, the exceptional quality of its early architecture still visible in the bones of gabled farmhouse and weathervaned barn; a fairy tale oasis hidden in a sun drenched ravine, enveloped by gently rising hillocks thick with wildflowers—tiger lilies, bluebells, flowering cactus in translucent yellows and pinks. Something about the place had seemed eerily familiar, as if visited once in a dream or some long forgotten childhood afternoon. Like a beloved, long departed aunt or grandfather it had embraced them, both of them—Alena is still certain of this—though Hamish had never been one to speak of such things out loud. But she had seen it on his face, in his eyes; had felt it deep within her and was satisfied that he had felt it, too. And as they'd stood there, silent, looking out over the surrounding, purple-tinged hills and deep green valleys shrouded in mysterious groves, breathing in air fragrant with the scent of wild roses that bloomed there, incredibly, in every possible shade from purest white to darkest crimson, she thought, but didn't utter for fear of breaking the spell: magic. No other place—and they'd been many in their years together—had ever affected the two of them at once in that way. Alena was certain it had invited them to return. Just as it had again today, invited them to stay. *Him* to stay. *Oh Hamish.*

The town of Sagebluff, if not ideal, was the closest in proximity to the magic they'd discovered. Set in a rugged valley, small and affordable, it had seemed the logical place to create a comfortable base from which to go exploring. And while those few months last summer had been brief, they'd been steeped in promise; Hamish had expressed a desire to set up a painting studio after several dry years. They'd brought nothing with them but a few clothes and some of Hamish's more easily packed sketching supplies and like newlyweds had embraced every little thing, ordinary or otherwise that they'd found to make the place a home. Items that others in their age group may well have scoffed at, bought as they were at garage sales or Mandy's Mandatories, the crazy little sprawling second hand shop at the end of the town's crumbling Main Street.

Though she doesn't really want it, Alena gets up and pours another cup of coffee, takes it to the porch and opens the screen door, steps out onto the small open deck and stands there breathing in the storm. She's grateful for the cool rush of air, heedless of the lashing rain on her skin as she gazes out at the electric light show beyond the shadowy, swaying trees. The lot next door to her right is vacant but next door to her left, she notices a light is on in the house and wonders who might have moved in; the place (like so many in these diminishing prairie towns) had been empty all last summer which had suited them, they'd been drawn to the area for, above all else, the possibility of calm and quiet in a world gone crazy and frankly, far too loud. She spots a man—forty, maybe—leaning against the exposed studs of a small, covered entryway, holding what looks like a beer bottle, talking to someone not visible, but with a distinctly feminine voice. She thinks she hears the soft murmur of a child, though it's hard to tell with the raging wind. So, a couple, maybe a family next door. Last year this would have bothered them, this potential invasion of their peaceful sanctuary. It bothers Rosalea now, but for completely different reasons. As she slips back inside, closes her door against the storm she wonders if, in the days—the years—to come, she will mind their presence.

ABOUT
THE WRITERS

THE WRITERS

PAT ABRAHAM is a Sydney-based writer. He writes best when given a deadline. He has been published in the Mascara Literary Review and Adas anthology, and long listed for the Furphy Literary Award.

Dr. KAREN LEA ARMSTRONG (she/her) is a writer and former family physician from Timmins, Ontario, Canada. Her publications include a novel (*Drownproofing*, 2023), nonfiction, short fiction, and poetry. She lives with her husband Paul and untrainable rescue dog Piper; find out more at www.karenleaarmstrong.com.

LIAM BOYLE lives in Galway, Ireland. Many of his poems deal with memory, family and heritage. He enjoys spending time with his grandchildren.

EILISH BRENNAN, an emerging Victorian writer, harnesses the power of words to evoke a sense of reflection on the shared experience that binds us. With each piece, she seeks to unravel the threads that tie humanity to the natural world, exploring the mysteries and wonders that surround us.

BRENDAN CALDWELL is a writer and journalist from Ireland. He was nominated for the Desperate Literature Prize in 2020 for his short story Omar's Ashes, and is published in the short story collection *Brevity Is The Soul Of Wit*. He writes regularly for gaming blog Rock Paper Shotgun.

BROOKS CARVER is a historical fiction writer, poet, and photographer who lives in Illinois. His novel *Give My Love to Ivey Rose* is set in the Tennessee hills and the Cherokee Nation of Oklahoma and his published anthology of short stories, poetry, and essays is called *Pilgrim Heart*. His poetry and short stories have appeared in numerous magazines throughout the country.

ANGELA COSTI is a poet and writer with a background in social justice and community arts. Her chapbook, *Adversarial Practice*, Cordite Poetry Review, was commended in the Wesley Michel Wright Prize 2024. Her sixth poetry manuscript, 'The Heart of the Advocate' will be published with Liquid Amber Press, March 2025.

SEAN CRAWLEY writes short stories, songs, non-fiction and the odd angry letter. He has three collections of short stories published by Ginninderra Press. Sean's desk is currently located in Long Jetty on the east coast of Australia.

JO CURTAIN is published in various anthologies and is editor of Geelong Writer's publication *Anomaly Street*. Jo's work often experiments with form and utilizes visual images. She weaves themes of personal experiences.

ADRIAN DOWNES is a recently retired architect/ designer, originally from the UK but has lived in Australia for 21 years, currently in Footscray, Melbourne. He has always harboured a desire to write fiction, and completing a couple of online creative writing courses ignited the spark to express himself and commit to writing on a regular basis. Adrian is interested in the human condition rather than particular genres and delights in the mundane details of everyday life and the misfits of society who surround us.

JANE DOWNING's stories and poems have been published around Australia and overseas, including in *Griffith Review, Big Issue, Antipodes, Westerly, Island, Overland, Meanjin, Cordite* and *Best Australian Poems*. Her novel, *The Sultan's Daughter*, was released by Obiter Publishing in 2020. She can be found at janedowning.wordpress.com

OWEN DWYER is a novelist from Dublin where his two books, the *Garfield Conspiracy* and *Number Games*, were published to great acclaim. Having spent thirty-five years building and running a business, he has now retired to concentrate on writing. He spends his time between Dublin and Italy, with his Italian wife. He has recently finished a new novel about Caravaggio, the original light and shadow man.

LEONE GABRIELLE writes in company of wilting roses and exhausted tea cups, from Seymour, a snaking river town on Taungurung country. Published: *Rochford St. Review, KalliopeX, Meniscus*. Leone also loves to knit socks, studies German and paints benches at her local park.

Dr **CHELINAY GATES** is an indigenous author, artist, playwright and Dr of Traditional Chinese Medicine. Intrigued by the soul's journey, her work explores the interface between the physicality and emotion of the environment into which we are born, juxtaposed to

life's teachers and lessons gifted to us so that we may cultivate our unique spiritual persona.

ALICE GORMAN is a space archaeologist and author of the award-winning book *Dr Space Junk vs the Universe: Archaeology and the Future*. She is a regular contributor to *The Conversation* and *The Best Australian Science Writing* anthology. Her poem 'Here now the Sun. A poem for Valentina Tereshkova, first woman in space', was selected for the Cambridge University Press anthology *Outer Space: 100 Poems* (2022). [PHOTO: BRENTON EDWARDS]

JENIFER HETHERINGTON lives on Wadjuk Boodjar, Western Australia, where she writes short fiction and poetry. Her work has been published in numerous journals and she is a participant in the Writing WA Emerging Writer's Programme. The ocean is her refuge in our troubled world.

EZ KNILL is an up-and-coming author born and raised on the Lefevre Peninsula, South Australia. They have a focus on poetics and magical realism, a keen interest in the beauty of the mundane, and a love for the atmospheric over the plot-heavy.

MAYA LE HER is an emerging British-Australian poet based in Sydney. Through a Dazed Open Call, her work was published in *Arlo's Art Therapy Journal*, a collaborative journal by Arlo Parks in support of CALM (Campaign Against Living Miserably). In 2024, her poem 'Persephone' won the Senior Original category of the Classical Association Poetry Competition (UK), she won the Senior Secondary Poetry category of the Mosman Youth Awards in Literature for the second time (AU) and she was named a Foyle Young Poet by the Poetry Society (UK).

TIM LOVEDAY is a writer, poet and an educator. He won the 2022 Dorothy Porter Poetry Award and the 2023 Venie Holmgren Environmental Poetry Award, and was a finalist in the 2023 David Harold Tribe Poetry Prize and 2024 Montreal International Poetry Prize. You can find out more at: timloveday.com.

K. JANE MAY's fiction publications include *The Fiddlehead*, *Grain*, *Pulp Literature* and *The Antigonish Review*. She took first place in the 2024 Lorian Hemingway Short Story Competition, was runner up in the 2024 Creative Writing NZ Prize, and placed second in both the 2019 Lorian Hemingway and the 2018 Sheldon Currie Prize. Jane currently resides in British Columbia, Canada where she is putting together a collection of short stories.

Born in Sri Lanka, SUZI MEZEI lives in Naarm on lands traditionally owned by the Boonwurrung People. Her work is published in Australia and overseas in journals and anthologies in print and online. It has been performed on stage and in podcast. She is currently working on a fiction collection.

G. M. MONKS' writing has appeared or is forthcoming in *riverSedge Literary Journal*, *The Militant Grammarian*, *L'Esprit Literary Review*, *Birdland Journal*, *The Hunger*, *Vine Leaves Literary Journal*, *The RavensPerch*, *Kansas City Voices*, and elsewhere. Awards with publication include finalist in Ben Nyberg Fiction Contest 2022, finalist in the 2020 Breakwater Review Fiction Contest, and runner-up in the 2016 Big Wonderful Press Funny Poem contest. Her debut novel, *Iola O*, was nominated for the 2020 PEN/Hemingway Award for New Fiction.

SOPHIE O'HAGAN is a MRes student at the University of York, her research centres around Percy Bysshe Shelley, temporality and Christianity. In her

fiction writing she draws from her life experiences and the natural world to address complex emotions and mental health, particularly PTSD.

ALEXANDRA O'SULLIVAN lives in regional Victoria, Australia. Her work has appeared in publications such as Meanjin, The Victorian Writer and The Guardian. She works as a high school English teacher and was recently included in the anthology *Teacher, Teacher*, published by Affirm Press.

OSHADHA PERERA is a poet and short story writer living in New Zealand. He is a winner of the Lancaster Writing Awards (Poetry), NZPS International Poetry Competition (Youth) and Southland Creative Arts Awards (Emerging Talent).

JAKE RICHARDS enjoys playing music, reading, gardening, and spending time in the outdoors. He enjoys creating imaginative stories for his three children and is excited to be sharing one with other people for the first time. Jake lives in Launceston, Tasmania with his family.

JEAN ROARTY lives in Dublin, Ireland. Her work has been published in various anthologies including Southword 38 New International Writing and, most recently, in the 2024 London Independent Story Prize anthology.

BELLA RONA completed her Creative Writing MA at the University of Birmingham. She was shortlisted for the Dinesh Allirajah Prize for Short Fiction 2021. She lives in London.

FRANÇOISE THORNTON-SMITH lives near the Grampians, Victoria, Australia, where she writes, reads, gardens and spends a lot of time as volunteer firefighter, with 20 years' experience of fighting bushfires. She is particularly interested in the relationship between nature and humans. She has been writing all of her life, and has won prizes in various local, national and international short story competitions.

VERONICA TROUP is an emerging poet who lives and writes on unceded Boonwurrung Country, in Naam/ Melbourne. Her work examines ideas of women, invisibility and place. She is currently writing her first poetry collection.

ROGER VICKERY has won numerous writing awards and his work has been published/ performed in several countries. In 2024 he won the Thunderbolt Crime Poetry Prize and was shortlisted for the Silver Gull Play Award, the Calanthe Poetry Prize and the Stringybark Times Past Award.

SCOTT WINKLER is a semi retired lawyer. He is a father, stepfather, grandfather, husband, brother and son. He has been writing short fiction in earnest for just 2½ years. During that time, his work has appeared on several long lists. One of his works, 'Winter Squall' was published in the *2024 Baby Boomers Plus Anthology* for authors born before 1966; and another entitled 'The Milky Way' won first place in the 2024 *Slippery Elm Literary Journal* prose competition sponsored by the University of Findlay, USA.